Totally Bound Publishing books by Cheyenne Meadows:

Wind Warriors
Tiger's Lily

I0570419

Wind Warriors

TIGER'S LILY

CHEYENNE
MEADOWS

Tiger's Lily
ISBN # 978-1-78430-143-9
©Copyright Cheyenne Meadows 2014
Cover Art by Posh Gosh ©Copyright July 2014
Interior text design by Claire Siemaszkiewicz
Totally Bound Publishing

This is a work of fiction. All characters, places and events are from the author's imagination and should not be confused with fact. Any resemblance to persons, living or dead, events or places is purely coincidental.

All rights reserved. No part of this publication may be reproduced in any material form, whether by printing, photocopying, scanning or otherwise without the written permission of the publisher, Totally Bound Publishing.

Applications should be addressed in the first instance, in writing, to Totally Bound Publishing. Unauthorised or restricted acts in relation to this publication may result in civil proceedings and/or criminal prosecution.

The author and illustrator have asserted their respective rights under the Copyright Designs and Patents Acts 1988 (as amended) to be identified as the author of this book and illustrator of the artwork.

Published in 2014 by Totally Bound Publishing, Newland House, The Point, Weaver Road, Lincoln, LN6 3QN, United Kingdom.

No part of this book may be reproduced, scanned, or distributed in any printed or electronic form without permission. Please do not participate in or encourage piracy of copyrighted materials in violation of the authors' rights. Purchase only authorised copies.

Totally Bound Publishing is an imprint of Total-E-Ntwined Limited.

If you purchased this book without a cover you should be aware that this book is stolen property. It was reported as "unsold and destroyed" to the publisher and neither the author nor the publisher has received any payment for this "stripped book".

TIGER'S LILY

Dedication

For my parents who have been supportive of this adventure the entire way. Thank you for believing in me and this dream.

Chapter One

Four forty-five. Fifteen more minutes before their extended Thanksgiving holiday began. Margaret, the receptionist, had dashed off right behind the final client of the day, eager to hit the grocery store and begin cooking for her large brood. The benefits and expectations of being a grandmother, she'd pointed out. That left Lily to clean and stock up after the harried day, while the doctor finished his notes.

Lily pulled the last bag from the trash can, adding it to her increasing pile to be taken out as she left work for the day. Mundane chores didn't care if she was a housekeeper or a nurse like she was—all part of the job. A job she was more than happy to have after her life had toppled like a deck of playing cards.

If there ever was an angel, Carson fit the bill. If he wasn't married, probably every woman in a fifty-mile radius would be banging on his door for some undivided attention from the handsome, smart, and friendly doctor. He radiated compassion and caring, working long and often late hours in order to see any client with a need—all his dedication along with a smile, kind word, and gentle hand. He'd given her a job when she had needed it most. For that, she'd happily spend the rest of her working life picking up the trash and whatever other task needed doing in his small practice.

Quickly, Lily tied up the final garbage bag, before stuffing a clean replacement in the plastic can near the back door while mentally checking off the closing routine chores.

The back door whined as it opened.

Spinning around, Lily saw a tall, dark-headed man step confidently through the back door, camouflage covering a powerful build. Her attention quickly moved from the man to the weapon he carried in his right hand. A rifle for sure, but not one used for hunting game. More like what she would expect someone in the military or even a SWAT team to use. Her heart raced as she kicked her stunned brain into action.

The newcomer's stark blue gaze quickly raked over the room before landing on her. His grim mouth, with a deep scowl, spoke of his current mood. Black smudges covered his face, sending her fear skyrocketing.

She opened her mouth to scream, only to find the strange man's hand immediately covering her mouth. His other arm wrapped around her middle, keeping her in place, facing away from him, but easily under his control. Instinctively, she began to struggle, kicking and pulling at his arm, anything to try to break free.

"Hold still. I'm not here to hurt you." The deep husky voice penetrated her brain.

That's probably what all the villains told their victims, lured them into a false sense of safety then did their worst. A momentary pause later, she renewed her fight.

He shook her a bit, the strong, tanned hand immobile over her mouth. "Stop it. I don't have time for this."

The sheer frustration and annoyance in his voice stilled her endeavors for release. That and the brute strength she felt in the body holding her told her that this man possessed the ability to do just about anything he wanted to her and there would be little she could do about it.

"Mayberry!" he shouted through the clinic.

Confused, Lily focused on breathing and searching for any opening to escape. *Mayberry? What did that mean?*

Carson strode quickly into the back room, coming to an abrupt stop when he spied the situation. A frown covered his face as he blinked a couple of times, as if trying to figure out some complex puzzle. His hands clenched into fists before his body stance relaxed. "Tiger?"

If the man acknowledged the name, Lily couldn't tell. Instead, she watched her employer's face, hoping that recognition meant a happy reunion, not a past of hatred. Her fear lessened as she heard her captor's voice once more.

"Sorry to barge in like this, Mayberry, but it's Dillon."

Immediately, Carson stepped forward. "Release my nurse and tell me what you need."

His hand loosened slowly along with the snug hold he had on her body. "No screaming." With that warning he set her free.

Without thought, she slammed her elbow back into the guy's gut, grumbling when he stepped away in the nick of time, only receiving a whisper of the impact.

"Damn she-cat."

She turned to glare up at the man who scared the living daylights out of her, even opened her mouth to give him a piece of her mind, but the doctor quickly interrupted.

"Dillon? What happened? Where is he?"

Both men hurried out the back door.

A minute later, they re-entered the room, supporting a man between them. They both wrapped an arm around him from each side, carrying him in a standing position.

Lily moved into action, clearing the path to the exam table, noting the state of the obviously injured newcomer. Close-cropped hair made the color difference between dark blond and sandy brown too difficult to call. Not quite as tall as the first guy, he still carried muscle and mass enough to impress. Both had scruffy whiskers, hinting at a few days without seeing a razor. Dust and dirt clung to his camouflage clothing just like the other man's with one major distinction. A large tear ran down the left thigh. Blood soaked the area, both fresh and dried.

Dillon, they'd called him.

He groaned as they laid him easily down on the exam table.

Lily raced for the bandage scissors, yanked them from the nearby drawer, and handed them over to Carson. As he cut the clothing, she dashed from cabinet to cabinet, gathering any supplies she thought might be needed. The men spoke softly in the background as she scurried around. Gauze, cleaning solutions, bandages, tape, and a sterile tray soon piled up on a nearby table, all within the reach of the doctor.

"How long ago was he shot?" Carson whispered across the space.

Tiger glanced at his watch. "Approximately fifteen hours ago."

"Damn." Carson continued with his work, cleaning and inspecting the wound. "Should have sought the nearest hospital, Tiger. This could be bad."

"Couldn't." The words rasped out of Dillon.

"Bullshit. Flash any of those high security clearance government passes that I know you both have. The locals wouldn't have batted an eye."

Everyone watched while the doctor worked in silence for a bit longer. He turned Dillon over, asked him a dozen questions, and studied the leg thoroughly before releasing a breath. "It appears like you're one damn lucky man, Bugle. I'll grab a quick X-ray to make sure. Good thing you have all this baby fat for that bullet to go through instead of important parts."

Dillon cracked open his eyes and snorted. "I'm not the one with the beer belly."

Carson chuckled. "Good thing I'm not either. It doesn't do to offend the guy caring for you, kid."

"Bugle?" Lily asked from her position beside the doctor, feeling a bit small and dwarfed by the surrounding men who were all a good head taller than she. She was all about average—average height, average build, just average.

Tiger snapped at her with his bright blue gaze from across the table, but he didn't speak.

She quelled the tremor running through her with such an intimidating expression aimed at her.

"Nickname. From years ago." Carson answered, using the saline to wipe away more of the blood and clean the wound, revealing the true injury underneath.

She recalled the name Tiger had called when he arrived. "Mayberry?"

"Don't ask." The doctor sent her a warm, reassuring smile. "I'll need more saline for irrigation, Lily."

She rushed off to the storage room to gather up three more bottles, clutching each to her chest as she made her way back to the patient. "And an IV. He needs fluids. Normal saline."

Before long, she had the IV going while the doctor stood to stretch out his back. "He needs antibiotics for a few days. Rest. Food, too."

Tiger glanced from Dillon up to the doctor. "Give me the antibiotics. I'll find somewhere to hole up. I've had basic medic training. Just get me the necessities."

Carson shook his head. "No. I mean he needs IV antibiotics. I don't think that pills are strong enough at this point to keep infection down. Besides, how are you going to lug all those supplies around with you, take care of your brother, and watch your back at the same time?"

"I've done it before."

"Not this time. Stick around here for a few days, rest and rehab." The corner of his mouth turned up, speaking when Tiger would have argued. "Doctor's orders."

They shared a long look before Carson spoke again. "Lily? You said you weren't doing anything but staying home over the holiday. These men need some nursing care…"

She stared up at Carson, her mouth dropping open. He wasn't saying what she thought he was saying? *Was he?* Even if she didn't have any Thanksgiving family dinner to attend, it didn't mean she wanted to take a couple of stray *Terminator* men home with her. "But... I... Don't they need a doctor's care?"

Dillon spoke up, pain lacing his voice. "Could be tails. Can't take risk. Cale can..."

Lily appraised the young man and her heart melted. He certainly needed looking after and attention. It wasn't his fault his brother possessed the manners of a bear with a thorn in his butt just out of hibernation.

"But..." Lily tried once more.

Carson held her gaze. "I would if I could. However, I can't get out of this visit with the family. Don't worry. I will just be a phone call away. I'll make sure you have everything you need. And"—he raked both men with a stern look—"they may be a bit rough around the edges, but they do know how to be gentlemen."

She glanced from Tiger to Dillon and sighed. Carson and his wife Casey had a newborn son, Adam, who happened also to be the first grandchild on both sides of the family. Carson had promised everyone weeks ago that they would spend the Thanksgiving holidays with the large family, savoring and sharing the adorable angel of a baby. Unfortunately, the grandparents lived several hours away, making it a long journey for the doctor and impossible for him to pop in each day to check on his patient. A small part of her mind picked up on an underlying deal sealer. If Dillon said people were after him, Carson would move heaven and earth to keep his young family safe. He couldn't turn his back on friends, but finding them a safe venue while they received medical care with someone he trusted would fit the bill to a 'T'. He had done so much for her. She simply couldn't refuse a favor in return. In the scheme of things, she owed him this and more.

A long sigh declared her decision. "Okay. Fine. But there has to be some ground rules."

"Of course."

"I have clean sheets, so please get Dillon showered before he lays on them. I don't have any food, since I was going to the store tomorrow, so I'll have to find time to do that. I'll need supplies and he certainly won't fit in my car."

"It will take me a while to get everything together." Carson seemed to consider her demands. "Go shopping now, but make it quick. Tiger and I will see to Dillon. I'll pull the IV antibiotics out of stock. We'll make it work." He nodded at her.

"One more thing." Lily's hands went to her hips as she frowned up at Tiger. "If they so much as upset my girls, there will be hell to pay."

"Girls? She has children?" Tiger asked, his attention directed to Carson.

He received a wide smile in return. "Something like that."

After spinning on her heels, she headed through the door to the office where her purse waited.

Chapter Two

An hour and a half later, Lily pulled into her driveway, already weary from the long day at work and shopping for two extra mouths to feed for a few days. *Big men with big appetites.* Luckily, the grocery store clerk, exhausted and bored, paid her little attention with her overflowing basket of food and items she could hardly afford. Her budget lacked the flexibility to allow for such luxuries. Yet there was no help for the situation. She had to feed them. Besides, everything usually came out in the wash. *Usually.*

The small two-bedroom stone house looked old and cozy from the road, nothing that people paid much attention to. However, it was home for her. A large covered front porch gave her space for a plant or three during the summer. Two bedrooms, two bathrooms, a kitchen, a living room, and a laundry room fit into the small square footage. As the house was over a century old, hardwood floors graced each room. Carson kept it in good condition and repair. After all, it was his home, one he allowed her to rent for a small monthly charge. All the appliances boasted energy efficiency and shiny newness down to the central air and heat. A fireplace made up the west wall of the living room, a necessity when the house was built, but a nicety now in case of power loss during a blizzard or ice storm.

Lily didn't have much furniture or belongings. A sleeper sofa and a small recliner sat quietly in the living room. Her king-sized bed filled the biggest of the bedrooms, the only real gift she had given herself after her mother's death. Not having a spare bed, she had turned the second bedroom into a storage room for linens and supplies. On the other hand, the kitchen held tools for baking, cooking, and canning. All the essentials were there. Though not luxurious or fancy, the house gave her comfort and peace, which counted for everything in her book.

Once she had put the car in the garage, she hastily grabbed up bags of groceries out of the trunk, carrying them through the door and into the kitchen while keeping an eye out for small escape artists. Not seeing any fur kids running around, she proceeded with a quick search and find mission, smiling when she found the two kittens curled up asleep with their mother on the living room couch. "Hello, Hope. We have company coming. I hope you don't mind. It's not like we had much of a choice, you see." When the calico lazily opened her eyes, Lily gently brushed her fingers over the cat's head. One black ear and one orange ear stood out starkly against the pristine white coat while her tail combined all three colors into a pretty blend.

She smiled softly then got busy, her mind still whirling from the earlier incident and the latest monkey wrench in a life seemingly full of the metal troublemakers.

Before this year, she'd lived happily in a suburb, working at a large hospital as a floor nurse and staying in a modest house with her mother. Her sweet, happy-go-lucky mother and best friend rolled into one, who loved life and living. Then, suddenly, her mother had grown ill. An aggressive form of pancreatic cancer, the oncologist had called it. They'd fought it with chemotherapy until her mother — her body thin and frail and racked with pain and nausea — had sadly shaken her head, declining any more treatment, instead wishing to die comfortably. The hospice had taken over her care and a week later, Lily's only living relative passed.

With her world turned upside down, Lily had made a hasty decision to start over. After all, nothing remained but memories and those had only seemed to drag her mood into the doldrums more often than not. She'd paid off the medical bills with money from the sale of their once-shared home, leaving her with little to survive on. A quick phone call and letter resigned her from her nursing position in the hospital. She'd packed and planned, all the while searching for a new job, a new lease on life.

In Cooperstown, she'd found just that. The small rural area consisted of hard-working farmers and down to earth people, with one family practice doctor in the area. Dr Carson Snider had happened to be searching for an office nurse. Lily's lucky stars had located the help wanted ad, taken her to his door, and landed her the position. The kind young doctor's generosity went much further. He'd moved her into his sole rental house at the edge of six hundred acres of prime pastureland where he raised cattle and horses in his spare time. Obviously guessing at her lack of funds, he'd made her a deal, namely low rent in exchange for watching out for the livestock, keeping their water tank full and clean, and checking the fences often for any needed repairs. Insisting she call him by his first name, Carson had become a good friend.

She'd taken a large pay cut compared to what she'd made at the hospital, but she'd felt the decision was right with every ounce of her being. The town, the people, the job—everything had called to her on a basic level. Peaceful and content described her feelings since moving here.

Her thoughts turned to the two men who would show up at her doorstep at any moment. Big and built, they appeared more like present-day warriors—soldiers of fortune, even. She'd read the intelligence in their eyes along with the firm resolve on their faces. They might be in a pinch at the moment, but they were nowhere near ready to toss in the towel. In fact, she doubted they knew the word 'quit'.

Tiger, the taller one, drew her focus. He'd scared the crap out of her earlier, for good reason, she understood now. Secrecy had obviously been needed in order to help his brother and provide for the safety of all involved. While she might not wish to repeat the scary experience, she could forgive his methods this once.

His image flashed through her mind as she absently unloaded the bags, storing the food in cabinets and the refrigerator, quickly and efficiently making use of the short time span before her company arrived. Tall, dark, and handsome—the old adage fit him. Even the smudged dirt couldn't take away from the muscular body hidden beneath camouflage fatigues. Hardness poured from Tiger, both in attitude and in sheer presence. The only hint of softness she could see revolved around his feelings for his brother. Externally, his full lips were the only feature that even began to come close. The rest of him made excellent eye candy if one ignored the intense scowl on his face. Predator. Dominant. Determined. Protective. All the words described the man she'd met just over an hour before. If one believed in past lives, she would bet Tiger took after his wild namesake—alpha, fearless, and territorial.

The more she considered Tiger, the more she realized two things. He demanded respect and came across as a bit off-putting. Yet, at the same time, something intrigued her about Tiger who just might snap her neck if she let anything happen to his injured brother.

She bit her lip, already worrying about the man with the gunshot wound. She had never been an emergency room nurse and honestly felt a bit in over her head caring for such injuries completely on her own. Carson had promised to be a phone call away. That certainly helped, but didn't add to her confidence much. At least she could email him pictures if things started to go downhill with the wound.

"I can do this. Besides, it's not like there's much choice." The spoken words offered her only a smidgen of comfort.

Dillon, they called him. Dillon and Bugle. A nickname, according to Carson. Interesting. She'd watched enough movies to understand that military personnel gave one another monikers on a regular basis—nothing unusual there. Yet, something tickled her curiosity. Ordinarily injured military men would be taken to the nearest military hospital for treatment. Not to mention, one shouldn't be running around in her quiet neck of the woods with such a wound to begin with. All the facts pointed toward something more.

A chill raced up her spine.

Her first Thanksgiving alone in the world and she'd been saddled with private nursing duty to gun-toting men who could probably snap her like a stick and bury her in the backyard with no one the wiser, with possible exception of Carson who wouldn't return for a few days. Too late to be of much help. *Wonderful.*

Once more she glanced at the small feline family and sighed. "It'll be okay. I promise." With that said, she scurried back to work, trying to beat the clock on her chores before the new roommates arrived.

Chapter Three

Tiger studied the small stone house with a keen eye. Years of survival training were hard to break as he immediately searched for faults and strengths in case of an emergency. Once a Navy SEAL, always a Navy SEAL. At least it looked sturdy and sound, should a firefight break out. He sure hoped not. Dillon needed rest and downtime, not dodging bullets on the run with a bum leg and his body fighting infection.

"We're here," Mayberry announced, turning the engine of the large SUV off. Tiger hopped out of the passenger seat, intent on getting his brother to the relative safety of a warm bed.

As before, each man took a side and carried Dillon to the garage door, ensuring no weight landed on his injured leg. The front door would have been closer and easier, but Tiger resisted the temptation. The large vehicle covered their silhouettes and the darkness should cover the rest. No sense in standing on a wide front porch with a light over their heads to announce their presence to the area. Too many years of survival training cautioned him into the shadows each and every time.

They entered the kitchen, Tiger steadying his brother while Mayberry shut the door behind them. Smells and noises instantly caught his attention. Pots sat on the stove, heating their contents while the sweet scent of cinnamon sent his hungry belly to rumbling. A washer nearby churned clothes and footfalls of the owner quickly approached.

She stepped out of the bedroom, still dressed in her work scrubs, minus the shoes. Blonde hair pulled back in a ponytail swayed with her movements. A classical beauty she wasn't. In fact, he had dated and been with much prettier women in his time. Yet something about this plain Jane caught his rapt attention.

"Let's put him in here." Lily gestured with her hands, indicating the bed's location.

A minute later, they eased Dillon onto the soft mattress, watching as he sank into the bed with a groan of relief. Freshly washed sheets, crisp and with a tinge of lavender, covered his brother's tired body.

Lily flipped the comforter over the linens, ensuring warmth and comfort.

Tiger couldn't help but smirk at the pastel floral decorations covering the matching linen. Men didn't complain about the scenery when in a lady's bed. If you were lucky enough to get there, you had more to grab your attention than artwork on cotton.

Lily's voice cut through his thoughts. "I've got some soup warming on the stove. Dillon, stay awake for a bit longer. Let's get your stomach full and something to drink, then I'll leave you to sleep as long as you like."

Dillon nodded, but his eyes remained closed.

Pulling his gaze from his little brother, Tiger addressed Mayberry. "I'll bring in those supplies."

"I'll help."

Together the two men traipsed back and forth bringing in medical equipment, medications, supplies, and personal belongings stored in two large duffle bags. Within moments, Lily had the room organized and headed to the kitchen.

Tiger watched her go, noting the gentle sway to her hips, before chiding himself for doing so. He'd learned the hard lesson about women a while back. In his opinion, most couldn't be trusted or depended on, not when something presumably more glamorous waved in front of their faces. "I'm not sure about this."

The doctor leaned over to check Dillon's bandage once more. They'd showered him at the office, placing him in spare scrubs that Carson had quickly cropped into shorts to allow air and easy surveillance of the wound. "I trust Lily. She'll take care of Dillon like a mother with her only child."

"It's not that…" Tiger began to explain, shutting his mouth when Lily reentered the room.

"Soup is ready. I found an old serving tray that I think will work for Dillon." She pinned Tiger with a stern expression. "I'll feed him if you want to eat and get cleaned up yourself. You can use the shower here." She pointed toward the bathroom to their right. "If you leave your clothes in the laundry room, I'll toss them in with mine."

"No need. I'll take care of it." He stood looking down at the woman whose crown reached not quite to his chin. Those hazel eyes flashed while her mouth thinned. She didn't like being told no. *Well, too bad. She can just get used to it.*

"Listen, macho, there is no sense in doing the laundry twice. It's a waste of detergent, water, and electricity. I guarantee my clothes contain no cooties and aren't contagious. So if you'll kindly dig out yours and Dillon's dirty clothes, I *will* wash them." She turned, then paused to look over her shoulder. "And before you think it, you are not walking around this house naked. My insurance doesn't cover counseling from the trauma of being surrounded by arrogant, naked Neanderthals." With that said, she strode confidently from the room.

A low chuckle sounded from beside him.

"Oh, shut up."

Carson shook his head. "Play nice with the good nurse, Cale. I would hate to have to kick your butt when I return."

"As if." Cale snorted in reply, somewhat irritated that Carson had dropped his real name into the conversation. He much preferred to keep the cute little nurse at arm's length. Using the nickname he earned in the Navy helped his cause—just another problem with this entire FUBAR mission, fucked up beyond all repair. He ran his hand through his hair and blew out a breath.

How did things go to shit so fast? More importantly, how was he going to fix them before an unexpected visitor arrived to finish what he started?

He caught sight of Lily as she puttered around the kitchen. Small yet fierce came to mind. Her work pants outlined a nice figure with curves in all the right places. A modest cleavage wouldn't inspire any *Playboy* readers, but the lack of an over-sized bosom didn't deter him in the least. Beauty tended to be only skin deep, covering selfishness and a downright cruel soul.

Once again he considered the sharp-tongued host. He made a point of looking all gift horses in the mouth — particularly Lily.

Lily carried the tray of soup, crackers, milk, and cornbread to Dillon's room. Tiger took it from her, dismissing her when she insisted on helping Dillon eat. Knowing a lost cause when she saw it, she left the room, following Carson as he headed toward the door.

"Call me if you need anything or have any concerns," he reminded her, stopping at the door in the kitchen.

"I will. Promise." She took a deep breath, feeling the panic well up. Biting her lip, she pasted a smile on her face. *What am I doing? Harboring criminals?* Living with men she knew nothing about who obviously resided just a single step on one side of the law or the other.

As if sensing her concerns Carson pulled her into a brotherly hug. Pushing back he kept hold of her upper arms, smiling reassuringly. "They may be rough, but they really are the good guys. I can vouch for that."

She nodded uncertainly.

His gaze flicked toward the bedroom before meeting her eyes once more. "They were comrades in arms a few years back. I trust them with my life. You are safer now than you have ever been."

The words slowly sank in, quelling most of the panic, but her nerves still crackled with adrenaline.

"Trust me."

She did trust him. The only reason she intended to go through with her promise — that and the fact that she really did owe him for everything he had done for her.

Tiger moved into her peripheral vision as he stepped from the bedroom. "What if Rambo here doesn't like something I do to his brother and shoots me?"

The corners of Carson's mouth crooked up. "Then Rambo gets to pack Mrs Snidley's pilonidal cyst next week."

That brought a smile to her face. Mrs Snidley had to be the most cantankerous, bitter, miserable, and hateful woman on the face of the planet. Nothing suited her, no one was good enough, and she complained mightily while the wound in her butt crack was packed. It couldn't have happened to a better person. She was a pain in the rear to everyone that had to deal with her, so it was only fair that she had a pain in her rear as well. *Gotta love karma.*

Lily gave Carson a warm hug, then shut the door behind him.

"Where do you want this?"

She turned to see Tiger standing with the tray in his hand. "I'll take it." Glancing over, she found the tray completely bare—not a scrap of food remained. She looked up at Tiger and arched her eyebrow, while lifting the tray from his hands.

"He fell asleep. I ate what he didn't finish."

"You need more to eat than that. Why don't you go to the kitchen and fix a plate? There's plenty and you guys look like you haven't had a good meal in a while."

"I'm fine."

The abrupt tone grated on her nerves, but she refused to let him get to her.

"By the way, what am I supposed to call you? If I'm calling your brother by his given name, don't you suppose I can call you something besides Tiger?"

His jaw ticked. "Cale."

She inclined her head. "Thank you. Now, if there's nothing else in the food department you might need, I'll work on that laundry."

He folded his arms over his broad chest as his light blue gaze stripped her bare. "I said I'll do it."

With a long sigh, she stood toe to toe with him. "Listen. If this is going to work, you're going to have to bend a little. I'm not asking you to be Gumby, just be civil and reasonable for a few days. That's it. A bit of cooperation might be nice, too."

Leaning down, he paused just inches from her face. "I'm a man who gets what he wants."

The stark promise stoked her ire. No way would she allow him to run right over her in her own home. Instead, she met his challenge and tossed back one of her own, "Yeah, well, I am woman, hear me roar."

He blinked at her as if stunned by such a declaration following his attempt to intimidate her.

Lily snorted, pivoted, then marched to the sink with the dirty dishes, quietly patting herself on the back along the way.

Chapter Four

Tiger watched her retreat with grudging respect. He could feel her nervousness, sense an innate deeply masked fear of him, yet she had stood toe to toe and thrown back the challenge in his face. Not many women had the gall to do that. At least not the ones he'd spent much time with. Those preferred their needs attended to be pampered, and tended to pout or get all defensive if he dared throw down a gauntlet. Not this one. She straightened her spine and spit out her demands.

Maybe nurses are tough creatures after all.

A quiet mewing caught his attention. Intrigued, he glided toward the small living room couch and peeked over. The sight of a mother cat nursing her two baby kittens set a small grin to his face. 'The girls', she'd called them. He recalled Lily's words about upsetting these particular creatures. He'd thought she'd spoken of children, not cats. Yet, somehow the sentiment remained the same, he'd wager, when it came to the little blonde. So protective of her ready-made family of felines. If a woman could be that caring and devoted to a small furry animal, perhaps she could and would care for his brother with the same determination and compassion. The thought alone eased tension from his shoulders and spine. *Perhaps this will work after all.*

No sooner had the idea hit than he quickly dismissed it with a bitter reminder of reality. In his experience, women were lazy and liked creature comforts and a man to care for their every need, using their wiles and bodies to gain power, money, and position. But when times got hard, they would quietly stab a guy in the back and move on to another gullible soul without a shred of remorse. He didn't have an issue with women. He simply understood the rules of the game. Sure, there were exceptions, but, like the chances of winning the lottery jackpot, they were slim to none. He'd been there before.

"Her name is Hope." Lily's quiet voice interrupted his thoughts.

"Hope?"

She nodded, her gaze lowering to the suckling kittens. "She showed up here one day. It was the end of July. Hot as blazes. The poor thing was so skinny and afraid." A moment passed before she continued on with her story, as if she were remembering the day with images in her mind. "I noticed her sitting beside the shed, half starved, and obviously in need. Not sure if she was tame, I quickly grabbed some lunchmeat and placed it in front of me. She looked at the food and cautiously moved up to eat it, hardly taking her eyes off me the entire time, as if she expected to be kicked or hit at any moment. I've never seen anything devour food as quickly or hungrily as she did."

He nodded, silently encouraging her to finish the story.

Lily reached out to lightly rub the head of the mother cat, speaking as she petted. "She let me touch her that day. Pet her. Soon I was able to pick her up and take her to the vet. It was touch and go for a while. Not only did she have an upper respiratory infection, which can be fatal in cats, but she had an abscessed leg as well. A bite wound from fighting for food, the vet guessed."

A loud purring sounded in the background as the cat expressed her enjoyment of the affection.

"So you brought her home?" Tiger prodded.

"Yes. The look she gave me when she first saw that lunchmeat in my hand, it was a look of sheer desperation. Of hope. As if I was the very last prospect she had on this earth. I couldn't just turn my back on that. I paid for the medications, bought the recommended high nutrition and calorie food for her, got her all fixed up as best as I could. Then I held her each night, talked to her, and let her sleep with me."

"And the kittens?" He gestured toward the babies. One black and white spotted kitten lay just under her mother's front leg while the other, an orange and white color, rested a bit farther back. Their little tails stood straight out from rounded bodies.

"She was too sick to get spayed when I first took her in to the vet. Then I worked so hard to get her well and put weight on her. By the time I realized she was pregnant, I didn't have the heart to spay her at such a late stage. Those babies deserved a chance too. The vet didn't think they would make it owing to the rough time Hope had while she carried them, but they proved him wrong." A smile full of pride appeared, making her face glow with affection.

"What are you going to do with the kittens?" Tiger reached over to tenderly run a finger over the soft coat of first one then the other.

"Why, keep them, of course." Lily glanced up, her voice full of conviction. "Faith and Charity will never be hungry or cold or suffer. Neither will Hope, ever again."

He braced himself, shaking off the softness and emotion the sad story evoked. More than one man had fallen for a pretty face and a tragic tale, only to be duped, taken for all they were worth, and left behind in the dust. It had happened to him once and he had vowed that never again would he or anyone he loved suffer for his miscalculations over a woman.

With one more touch to the babies, he headed toward the bedroom, needing distance from the woman who tugged at his heartstrings with her tale of compassion. She might be a savior for the furry forms lazing on the couch, but he knew better. The past lived for a reason. "I'm going to take that shower. Make sure nothing happens to Dillon or there will be hell to pay."

"Ignore him. He's old and has forgotten what little manners he ever learned."

Lily turned toward the tired voice coming from her bed. She'd come in to check on her patient after Tiger had departed for the shower. Deep brown eyes contrasted with the blond hair standing straight up from his buzz cut. A friendly grin beckoned her. Such a contrast to the severe frown from Cale minutes earlier.

Dillon had so far proved to be the more likable brother. He smiled. He thanked her. He never once threatened her with doom. Of course, she'd known him for a handful of hours, so all that could change. "I fear a mere sneeze out of you and he'll rush back in, declare me a witch and to heck with finding a stake. He would simply shoot me on the spot and toss my body out the back door for the coyotes to nibble on." She moved to the edge of the bed.

"He wouldn't dare harm a hair on your head," Dillon tried to reassure her.

She nodded. "He's a bear? Somehow I had already guessed that." Deliberately, she went for silly, trying to keep the conversation light and earn a chuckle from her patient.

Dillon grinned widely at her teasing. "Definitely a bear most days."

"As surly as a bear with a toothache, that is. Pretty to look at from a distance, but deadly if you get too close."

"A nurse with a sense of humor. I never knew such existed," he tossed out, shifting his sore leg carefully.

Tugging the covers to lay neatly over her patient, Lily joined in his fun. "A man with humility and a brain. How rare."

Warm chuckles carried across the room before Dillon's amusement turned serious once more. "Really, there is no need to be afraid of him. He's gruff, but he can be kind."

"Me? Afraid of him?" Lily clutched her chest while pasting an expression of mock horror on her face. "No. Don't tell me. He's addicted to that big purple dinosaur. Oh, dear me, say it isn't so. My sanity won't survive hours and hours of those videos. And those songs. Yikes."

Dillon burst out laughing at her dramatics. "You're funny."

The small success bolstered her spirits. "Why, thank you. I do try. Patients need more than just medical care, you see. Entertainment is at the top of their list." She smiled warmly down at him, feeling at ease, and glad that she had accepted the task of looking over him until he healed enough to be on his way once more. She genuinely liked Dillon and felt an easy connection with him, like instant friendship. Considering the hasty plans and the invasion of her house by two men she knew by first names only, that said something.

She blew her bangs out of her eyes and sighed. If only his brother could smile and tease and act like a normal human being. If only pigs flew, too.

"You remind me of Della, my fiancée." Dillon's eyes reflected happiness along with something akin to longing.

Lily didn't miss Dillon's obvious love for the girl. The corner of her mouth curled up at his words. "She must be something special to have corralled you."

He chuckled. "I'm the lucky one. She's an angel."

"I'm happy for you. While I don't know diddly about you guys, I can see kindness in you. You deserve happiness in life."

"Don't judge Cale too harshly. There're reasons for his behavior." Dillon tilted his head. "Maybe he just needs someone like you to soften his edges, just like Della did with me."

Lily put her hands up. "Oh, no. Not me. I prefer to avoid any swift boots sending me flying to the back forty, thank you very much."

Dillon adjusted his pillow and chuckled. "I didn't take you for a chicken."

She rolled her eyes. "Bok. Bok." After a moment, her amusement faded. "Don't worry. I'll play nice with Cale."

"Just to show him how it's done?"

"Bingo."

As if he had heard their conversation, Cale chose that moment to emerge from the shower, towel-drying his cropped hair while wearing a pair of sweats. His gaze roamed over her and Dillon as she still sat on the edge of the bed. Yet, the moment Cale appeared tension once more blanketed the room like a heavy rain cloud just waiting to drop a bucket load of hail.

"Flirting will get you nowhere with him. He has a girlfriend, a good woman, waiting for him at home." A stern glare followed.

Lily's good mood vanished like a water puddle in the midsummer heat under the harsh lash of Cale's tongue. "I know. Her name is Della and they are hoping to marry next spring."

If he was stunned by her knowledge, he didn't show it. A slight flicker of light across those blue eyes revealed nothing. He watched her pat Dillon's hand, then stand. "And quit pining for the doctor. He's already taken. Or does that even matter to you?"

A gasp escaped at his accusations.

"Cale!" Dillon sat up, growling at his older brother, arm reaching out to interject.

Lily waved at the younger Dillon, giving him a quick smile of reassurance. She could handle the situation and those gruff accusations. For a long moment, she debated the wisdom of arguing with the hyena, but decided enough was enough. "Listen, soap for brains, I'll have you know that I have no romantic interest in Carson." A snicker sounded from the bed as Dillon reacted to her name-calling. Ignoring it, she plunged ahead. "He's a friend, a very good one, and one that I will be forever grateful to for helping me when I needed it the most."

Tiger stood tall and glared down at her. "Don't give me that shit. I saw the way you looked at him when he left and the hug you gave him. Call it what you want, but your actions say different."

Stomping her foot in agitation, Lily stepped forward, nearly snarling at the cranky brother. "I look at him as a mentor, a person I admire and respect. Yes, I care for the man. Like I would a brother or a close friend. Hugs are allowed among friends if both parties are amenable to the affection. I adore his wife. In fact, we're best friends. If you don't believe me, call him up and ask. Or, even better, call up Casey. She'll set you straight."

Shooting him another glare, Lily left the room before she did something dire like kick the man in the shin and end up tied to the front door as a consequence of messing with the ogre and losing. Besides, piles of laundry called. She needed to make the sofa into a bed for the night, the cats had yet to be fed, and tomorrow's meal preparation started today. Unfortunately, none of those chores would do themselves.

Chapter Five

Lily woke with a purring sound and a paw patting her face. Blinking, it took her a moment to recall that she had slept on the sleeper sofa in the living room as Dillon occupied her one and only bed. Her glow in the dark watch that she purposely wore to bed read a few minutes past five.

"Let me guess. You and the babies are hungry again?" Automatically, she stroked her fingers over the calico's face and down her back. She had learned a while ago that sleeping wouldn't happen if Hope had other plans. The cat ruled the house and all its occupants whether she knew it or not. Who was she kidding? Hope realized that fact and ruled regally. With a sigh, Lily climbed out of bed, heading for the kitchen and canned cat food. At least Hope seemed to have taken the invasion in her stride. She didn't appear nervous or pensive with the appearance of the guys. With any luck, it would stay that way. She had worked too hard and spent more than she could afford to get that cat back to a healthy state. No way would she let anything interfere with that now.

"Brrrr." Rubbing her arms, she made a quick stop at the thermostat, turning the heat up a bit. She purposely kept the setting low to help ease the electric bill owing to her strained budget with the record low temperatures they were experiencing this November. But she really couldn't expect to freeze her guests, either. With a sigh, she grabbed up breakfast for her small brood.

No sooner had she opened the cans than the kittens, along with their mother, dashed over to busily inhale their early morning breakfast. The high calorie canned kitten food cost an arm and a leg each time at the vet's office, but she couldn't refuse them. Not when they obviously loved the stuff. Even though she kept a large bowl full of dry kitten morsels, they much preferred the wet food—like a kid faced with eating broccoli who ate everything else first. Taking a moment to watch the furry family, she sighed with quiet pleasure, then glanced back at the clock on the kitchen wall. "Time for antibiotics."

She walked over to the tiny spare refrigerator that Carson had brought that held the IV antibiotics. Upon selecting the correct variety, she carried it quietly into the bedroom.

Dillon slept on his right side, curled up to face the door. He looked like a teenager, a 'baby face' people would call him. Way too young to be in such a dangerous profession—although his physical features told a different story. The linens halfway covered him, revealing his borrowed scrubs that did little to hide his body, especially with the pant legs cut off. Large and obviously powerful, he rivaled Cale in brute mass, not like a bodybuilder, but more like a powerful man used to hours of manual labor each day. Strength born out of the life he led instead of working out in a controlled gym setting.

She easily saw why Della had chosen Dillon—his looks, his easy smile, and pretty face. Put those together and most women would eagerly line up for a chance at him.

Glancing over, she found Cale asleep on his other side in the large bed, his back to his brother. Sweats covered his bottom half while a black matching T-shirt completed the package she could see around the thick bed comforter. He, too, bore the look of an athletic, fit male in his prime. No one could miss the bulging muscles and ease of movement he'd shown before, like a talented athlete well versed in the actions of his body.

Her focus lifted. A square jaw promised stubbornness to the nth degree while sharp angles created a particularly masculine face, much like the work of a superb sculptor. Not as youthful, innocent, or beautiful as Dillon's features, but more rugged. Short dark brown hair added an interesting contrast to his light blue eyes. Once he lost the continuous scowl in rest, Cale appeared all the more handsome and approachable. *If only he smiled.* A twinge of sadness washed over her at the thought of Cale never cracking a grin. Life was too short to not share laughs now and again.

She had offered him the sleeper sofa last night, which he'd immediately declined, refusing to leave Dillon. Not that she blamed him. She'd also pointed out that the king-sized bed had more than enough room for them both. There was no sense in sleeping on a cold hardwood floor when he didn't have to. He must have agreed considering his position at the moment.

Lily quietly moved to the IV pump. The only one owned by the small clinic and a necessary tool for her. An alarm would sound if the fluids ran out or if there was a problem with his IV line. So much better than just running everything on gravity like the old days. Half the time the fluids would slow down allowing the plastic needle in Dillon's arm to clot off, or, just the opposite, it would run really well and the bag would be empty in no time. Trying to keep a continuous set amount going on a gravity drip was never easy or exact.

"It's just me, Dillon. Time for your next antibiotic. I'll just get it going and let you sleep," she whispered, afraid of startling him awake with her close presence. Military types and men of war probably had built in reflexes to take someone down if not completely out if they got too close when a man snapped awake. She'd cared for more than one war veteran in her hospital nursing career. Most were good guys still carrying deep wounds. Typically, they warned her to stay away until they were good and awake for her own safety. She could only presume the ideology carried over to this situation as well.

Dillon mumbled but didn't bother to open his eyes. She smiled, but quickly went about putting the syringe full of medication on the machine and programming it to infuse. That task complete, her attention fell to the other man in the room once more.

"Nice pajamas," Cale muttered from his side of the bed.

Lily blinked, a bit surprised that he was not only awake, but that he had addressed her. Cale probably slept like a wolf, waking up with each and every sound and motion. *Predator.* The billing fit him.

She glanced down at her robin egg blue pajamas covered with animated kittens in all shapes, sizes, colors, poses, and activities, and shrugged. They were comfortable, and who didn't like kittens? The hoarse words could have been either amusement or sarcasm. She opted for the former. "Thanks."

When no further comments followed, she tiptoed out of the bedroom, heading for the kitchen to get an early start on her baking.

* * * *

A couple of hours later, she finally heard rustling coming from the bedroom. Pulling the freshly made cinnamon rolls from the oven, she called over her shoulder, "Your clothes are clean and hanging in the laundry room. Breakfast will be ready in fifteen minutes."

No one answered her, but she caught a glimpse of Cale in sweats striding through the house, presumably looking for suitable day clothing to wear. She'd done the very same thing not too long ago, pulling on old worn jeans and a sweatshirt—warm and comfortable.

She set about preparing breakfast, fixing a large batch of scrambled eggs, toast, and sausage, having absolutely no idea what they liked or wanted to eat. Since the whole world minus her seemed to require coffee in the mornings, she set the unused java maker in the corner to working with the flavored variety she had picked up the day before on impulse. Some people remained cross and as sociable as a crocodile with a sore tail until they had a few cups of the strong liquid.

A loud grunt sent her dashing around the corner. The scene had her skidding to a halt and hollering, her lungs clenching in panic. "The babies!"

Dillon wobbled on crutches still wearing the scrubs he had gone to sleep in last night, trying to negotiate a path to the kitchen while avoiding the six week old kittens under foot. "Watch it!" he called down to them, listing heavily to his injured leg side, but they simply swatted at his foot.

Deftly, Cale reached around Dillon's leg, scooping the girls out of danger's way while wrapping an arm around his brother's waist, stabilizing and steadying him until Dillon regained his balance. The metal pole holding the IV pump stopped where Cale released it.

"Thanks, bro."

"No problem."

Dillon continued on his way, the path now cleared of any obstacle that might impede his progress.

Once Dillon had made his way to the kitchen, Cale gently set both kittens on the floor, giving them a quick stroke down each of their backs.

Lily breathed a sigh of relief, thankful for Cale's quick hands and thinking. Otherwise, Dillon could have taken a harsh fall or one of the kittens could have been stepped on, or worse. She didn't want to think about that. Instead, she pasted on a cheery smile. "I didn't expect to see you up and out of bed so soon."

A bit out of breath, Dillon hobbled to the nearest chair, pulled it out, and plopped down loudly. "I need to get moving. Can't lay around in a bed all day. Not if I want to get better."

"True. But, don't push yourself too hard. Okay? I don't want you to suffer a setback."

Cale pulled out the seat beside his brother. "He needs his butt kicked, not babied." Unlike Dillon, Cale dressed in all black, an outfit Lily had washed when they had arrived.

Recognizing the now familiar crankiness from Cale, Lily chose to ignore his harsh words. Instead, she turned back to the stove then proceeded to set the hot meal before them. "I wasn't sure what you guys wanted or liked. And I have homemade cinnamon rolls, too."

Dillon shoveled some eggs on his plate, then stabbed a sausage round, sticking it in his mouth. "This is wonderful."

"I guess I did okay, then." She smiled slightly, unashamedly asking for a compliment in her need to ease the slight tension in the room. Not entirely awkward, the silence lacked warmth.

Both men nodded, too busy eating to talk.

Lily took the remaining chair before absently placing food on her own plate. With such broad-shouldered and big-boned men, Lily felt a bit like a gazelle amidst a whole herd of wildebeest. Not that the men were ugly and scruffy, quite the opposite. Strong chins, sharp eyes, and pronounced bone structure spoke of good genes and high intelligence. They were more like the alpha lions of a pride than shaggy hoofed wildebeest.

A soft squeak broke the silence. Cale looked down by his leg. "What do you want, cat?"

Lily glanced under the table. Hope had decided to visit, standing with her front legs on Cale's leg, outright begging for food. "She doesn't care for eggs, but would probably eat the sausage." Pretty much any time Lily cooked, Hope made sure to check out the tidings, eating what she liked, and sticking her nose up at the rest. For an animal nearly starved to death three months ago, she now proved downright picky, walking away from foods typically craved by cats including the famous favorite feline treat—tuna.

Without hesitation, Cale grabbed his paper towel, cut up a lump of meat, and placed it on the floor. The cat immediately dove in, chewing with gusto.

Dillon smiled at the scene to his left. "Eats you out of house and home, huh?"

"You have no idea." Lily shook her head with a small grin. Her babies might be spoiled but they were happy and returned her adoration tenfold in the form of companionship and entertainment.

"Doc said you didn't have any plans for Thanksgiving?" Dillon asked between bites of his scrambled eggs.

Surprised, she stared at Dillon.

He grinned. "I was shot in the leg. Nothing wrong with my ears."

She returned his expression before sobering. Setting her fork down, she took a moment to wipe her mouth with the towel. "My mother passed away in February of this year. I don't have any other living relatives."

Cale looked over his plate at her, but remained mute.

Dillon's mouth pinched in concern. "I'm sorry to hear that."

"Thanks."

"Your father?"

"He was killed in the line of duty as a beat cop. Bank robbery gone bad." Her voice fell flat at the blaring reminder of how alone she really was in the world.

"How old were you?" Cale's deep drawl entered the conversation.

"Fourteen."

He gave a swift nod. "That explains the Glock in the top drawer of your nightstand."

Not completely surprised, Lily released an exaggerated gasp. She couldn't find the energy to get upset over Cale checking out her place thoroughly. She'd probably have done the same thing if it came down to a sibling's safety. "You fondled my underwear? Isn't that some sort of fetish or perversion or something?" She fought back a smile, but lost.

Dillon chuckled. Cale's lips twitched.

Lily rolled her eyes at him, enjoying the byplay and thawing of his frozen demeanor. "I don't think you'll fit in my undies. Besides, I'm not sure baby ducklings and bunnies are quite your style."

Dillon cracked up. Cale released a snort followed by an amused chuckle, the grin making him all the more handsome.

Lily smiled to herself at the small victory and major accomplishment in her book, but dared not delve too deeply into her motives for trying to get this particular man to experience happiness in life. He would only be around a few days then return to his high-secret, high-stress world. Any cracks she made in his steel resolve would surely seal shut as soon as they went their own way. *So, why am I even bothering? Because I can't stand to see him suffer.*

"What about you guys? Any family?" Unsure what they could or would share, Lily threw out the generic question. "Have any pets that rule your life?" She glanced at Hope who sat on her haunches, licked her lips, and meowed at Cale once more, receiving another tasty reward for her efforts.

Cale took the lead on this one. "Parents, yes. Demanding pets, no."

Biting her lip, Lily tossed out another pitch. "Underwear fetish?"

Those light blue eyes sparked with emotion while the corners of his mouth curved upwards in a teasing grin that stole her breath. Gorgeous. Absolutely gorgeous.

"Wouldn't you like to know?"

The words threw her for a loop nearly as much as the bright smile had. Never had she imagined she'd see such an expression, much less be the recipient of his smooth attempt at flirting. The low timbre of his voice plucked at deep nerves, causing her belly to do a slow summersault. Her world jiggled then quickly righted itself with newfound knowledge and appreciation.

Lily's face heated as she began to fan herself with a free hand. Both men laughed at her obvious embarrassment. Still, she couldn't help her reaction.

"Heathens." She muttered under her breath, taking a sip of juice to hopefully cool down a bit.

One simple smile turned Cale from taciturn drill sergeant into a living, breathing Adonis who stirred something deep inside her that had remained dormant for as long as she could remember. Passion. Need. Want. Finally, a man who garnered her attention and made her feminine parts sit up and take notice.

All for a man who would walk away and never look back.

Just her terrible luck.

Chapter Six

Dillon sat back with a sense of wonder listening to his older brother spar with the young nurse. For the past few years he'd rarely seen anything resembling the wry sense of humor Cale had possessed as a kid. Life had beaten it out of him. Yet, here they sat, in an old stone house in the middle of nowhere, eating cinnamon rolls, feeding table scraps to an already plump cat, and Cale smiled and laughed, reminiscent of the days of old. Dillon caught a glimpse of the old Cale, the one he hadn't seen in forever.

Not for the first time, Dillon cursed the evil witch known as Rachel. Anger rolled his stomach at just the whisper of that name. The woman who'd yanked Cale around by his love handle and ended up burning him every chance she'd gotten. The divorce had proved drawn out and particularly nasty, but at least there had been no children to fight over. Rachel had refused to have any, citing that she didn't want to become fat and ugly as she'd believed other women did after bearing children. How his brother could have loved that fucking pile of shit woman remained a mystery to everyone. All she had cared for was herself, her clothing, and spending every penny Cale could bring home on nonsensical baubles. Cale had risked life and limb each day just to keep that bitch in the manner she'd demanded. An absolutely useless human being, in his opinion.

After the divorce had wrapped up, Cale had thrown himself into his work, taking the most dangerous jobs in their private sector para-military specializations. Dillon worried often that Cale would get himself killed one day. At the pace and aggressive levels he'd lived at for the past two years, it seemed almost inevitable. But, money wasn't worth the life of his older brother and that was a sure fact.

In all honesty, he wanted to move on to another career, somewhere more stable and safe where he and Della could settle down and raise a family. Riches weren't required, just enough to keep them going— the American dream. His dream didn't include looking down on a compound with the scope of his sniper rifle, patiently waiting for all hell to break loose. No. Deep down, he knew this was his last mission. No longer did he have the dedication or desire to keep tackling the scum of the earth, never knowing when he would eat, rest, or die. When a man lost his edge and want for such a life, then he ended up getting himself and others killed. Thus, it was time to get out. Della deserved a husband by her side and a father to the kids he hoped to one day have.

"Got any other fetishes I need to know about?

Cale arched an eyebrow. "Such as?"

Lily shrugged. "I don't know. Some odd sexual attraction to cows, perhaps? Or the uncontrollable need to lick people's bare feet while they sleep."

"Cows, no. Licking..." he leaned closer, "is a possibility."

Her eyes widened. "Oh my God. You have a thing for feet?" She scrunched her nose up.

"Did I say I licked feet?"

Confusion covered her face. "Well, not exactly."

Cale sat back. "I'd rather lick a creaming woman's..."

Lily coughed. Dillon whacked her on the back, shooting a scolding glance toward his brother, only to find Cale chuckling in obvious enjoyment of Lily's naive reaction.

Realization clicked. By some stroke of good fortune, they had been thrown into Lily's life and home. His brother, for the first time in years, was relaxed and actually bantering with a woman, his surly attitude solidly on the back shelf this morning. *Promising.*

After thinking for a long moment, Dillon formulated the beginnings of a plan. It could be the answer he'd sought for the past couple of months, each time he had considered walking away from his present career.

He'd worried Cale would spiral downwards, throwing caution to the wind without Dillon to watch his back. Now, perhaps another stable force could pull Cale from the fires of his ravaged heart and return him to the man he used to be. Nothing would please Dillon or appease his need to protect his brother more than watching Cale transform into the goofy brother he recalled in his memories.

I'll make it work.

"Why do they call you Bugle?" Lily's question pulled him back into the conversation.

He opened his mouth to speak, but Cale beat him to it. "He looked like a young, smooth-faced kid that had never once used a razor on his face. Like the bugle boys the army used to have during the Revolutionary War."

"And what did you call Carson? Mayberry?"

"He's from a small rural town where no one locked their doors and everyone knew everyone else's business."

Lily took a sip of her juice, then met Dillon's gaze. "He won't tell me, I'm sure. Why do they call him Tiger?"

Cale glanced warningly at him, but Dillon only grinned mockingly in return. "Oh, there could be a few explanations for that."

"It's because I stalk my prey and hunt alone," Cale tossed out, his voice gruff with irritation.

Dillon leaned in close enough to stage whisper to Lily. "Personally, I think it's because, like most cats, tigers can lick themselves."

Lily tittered. Dillon yelped when Cale kicked his shin under the table.

"Brat." Cale shook his head, but couldn't suppress the bright flash of amusement in his mind.

Yes, definitely worth a try. Sinking his teeth into a hot roll, Dillon couldn't restrain the low moan of pleasure the pastry brought to his taste buds. "Oh, man." Sweet and hot, the treat nearly melted in his mouth. Granted, he hadn't eaten homemade cinnamon rolls in years, but this was simply a taste of heaven.

An echoing sound of pleasure mimicked his own. Cale closed his eyes and savored the first bite, obviously agreeing wholeheartedly with Dillon's own assessment. "You can certainly cook, I'll give you that."

Lily beamed at the praise. "My mother worked at a bakery for years. She taught me how to make all kinds of things."

Dillon met Cale's eyes and smiled to himself. The way to a man's heart was rumored to be through his stomach. If anyone could get to Cale, it would be Lily and her decadent desserts. But, sometimes, even miracles needed a helping hand. One he was more than prepared to lend.

Chapter Seven

An angry hiss carried across the space, filling in the companionable silence following breakfast.

Lily turned from the dishwasher where she was busily stacking dirty dishes. "Oh, boy. Here we go again."

Cale glanced over to the living room, watching the small kittens arch backs, growl, and pounce toward one another. In a matter of seconds, Faith jumped on top of Charity and the wrestling match began. Tufts of fur flew as the girls dove in, trying to pin the other down, gain the advantage, and win the present skirmish.

Feeling eyes on him, he glanced down to find Hope staring up at him with an expression of patient annoyance that seemed to say, 'See what I have to put up with?' Giving her a quick commiserative scratch behind the orange ear, he stood, dutifully carrying his coffee mug to the sink.

Lily's antics this morning hadn't gone unnoticed by him. In fact, he had found himself relaxing, opening up, and actually enjoying the morning meal with her.

She gave as good as she got, even as she blushed crimson red at his lighthearted bantering.

Innocent.

He'd bet his last clip of shells she'd never been with a man. Cute and peppy, she stood out as a novelty to him. After all, his brushes with the fairer sex these days revolved around one-night stands and a hot fuck here and there. With his intense schedule and lack of interest in another long-term commitment, he didn't have the time, patience, or interest in spending weeks or months wooing and dating a woman. Instead, he much preferred to get down to the basics — pump and dump then move on.

Once more he studied Lily and mentally shook his head. No, he didn't have the least experience with her kind. That didn't stop his cock from standing at attention as she had stared at him earlier that morning while he and Dillon had rested in bed. Each place her eyes had touched felt like a tiny caress, enough to stimulate his libido and waken his desire.

Maybe if things were different, he'd consider taking her to bed and initiating her. Just as well Dillon stood as a buffer, because he needed to keep his sights on the ultimate goal — getting out of there before they were caught in a trap — and finish the original mission before Lansing could hurt anyone else. A tall order, but not impossible.

One small detail bugged him. By leaving, would they put Lily at risk? Cale's chest tightened at the thought.

From what he'd witnessed thus far, she deserved better than to have danger fall on her head for his and Dillon's sins. Protective instincts rose. "What do you have to do today?"

After taking the cup and sliding it on the top shelf, Lily closed the dishwasher door before answering his question. Her gaze found Dillon. "Give him another antibiotic and change his dressings. Oh, Carson said for him to sit in the bathtub if he can manage it. It will clean out his wound more."

Cale followed her gaze, noting the lines of pain on his brother's face along with the fatigue in his dull eyes. The slight activity this morning had worn him completely out. "His belly's full now. I'll get him something for pain then get him back to bed for a nap."

"I keep telling you guys I'm not deaf." Dillon frowned up at them. "And I don't need anything for pain. I'm fine."

Cale opened his mouth to disagree, then quickly shut it. More than once he'd stood where Dillon now stood, and nearly every time had refused pain medications. Soldiers needed a clear head, no room for a cloudy judgment in his line of work—too many lives at stake. Besides, pain was a common occurrence to be shrugged off most of the time. "Fair enough. But I think the nap is certainly in order."

Dillon didn't protest.

Once more he prodded Lily. "What else do you have to do?"

She pushed the start button on the appliance before turning to meet his eyes. "I have to fill the water tank for the livestock, walk the fences to check for breaks or down wire, finish the laundry, and set a pie shell and frozen berries out to make a pie."

"Livestock?" He knew cattle and horses grazed in the pastures behind the house—that fact came from his quick surveillance of the place. But his gut told him she didn't have the money or time to care for large animals, nor the land to harbor them on.

"Carson's. This is his rental house," she hastily explained while wiping down the kitchen table with a damp rag. "In exchange for a lower rent, I make sure they have plenty of water, check the fences around the house, and do head counts."

That puzzle piece snapped into place in his head. No wonder she idolized her boss. Not only did he give her a job, but he provided a roof over her head and a manageable way of paying rent without busting her limited budget too. He could easily understand the low wages encountered in a small town doctor's office that existed off poor insurance reimbursements. If major hospitals struggled with finances, this area had to feel the strain all the more. He credited Carson greatly for finding alternative ways to supplement her income without breaking his business bank account.

If the woman had money, nothing he could see hinted in that direction. He would say in absolute faith that she simply made ends meet with not a lot of flexibility in that tight belt. "I'll go with you."

"You don't need to. I do it every day."

"I want to check things out, just to be sure." His tone discouraged argument. He could see Lily struggle with the need to ask more questions and the curiosity behind her eyes, but she wisely kept her mouth shut. *Smart woman.* "After we get Dillon back to bed before he falls asleep at the kitchen table."

When Dillon didn't argue, Cale moved to help him up, giving the extra strength and stability needed until the younger man could get his crutches back under him. Lily grabbed the medication from the small fridge, jumped over to grasp the pole, and agilely pushed it behind them as they made their way slowly but surely back to the bedroom.

By the time they'd finally gotten him settled and under the covers, Dillon's eyes were closing as his breathing evened out. The quick sleep showed the level of exhaustion he suffered. Cale studied his brother's face with worry, noting the paleness and deep sagging under his eyes. His gut clenched in guilt, knowing that if he hadn't pushed so hard, Dillon wouldn't be lying there suffering now.

Maybe it's time to find a new career? As soon as the thought struck, he quickly dismissed it. *What else would I do? Sit at a desk all day and watch my ass grow wider? Not in this lifetime.*

By the time he pulled on his thick black jacket, Lily had attached the antibiotic, punched some buttons, and headed to her closet before tugging out an old ragged quilt material coat. His former wife wouldn't have been caught dead in such a thing, scoffing it for being something that a street person might pick up from the Goodwill Store — the same with Lily's hand-me-down scarce furniture in the house. Absolutely nothing he saw spoke of money or the wish for expensive things. In fact, the only article that appeared fairly new was the white tennis shoes she wore to work. Lily gave everything else a second life, making them work the best she could instead of replacing them. It only drove home the idea of how different the two women were and the simple fact that Lily didn't have much, but not once did he hear her complain about her station or lack of monetary resources. Almost any other woman he'd ever known would've lamented and whined about their lot in life. Not Lily.

Not yet. He quickly reminded himself. He had known her less than twenty-four hours and his instincts weren't always right. The majority of the time, yes, but in his field of work, 'almost' could easily get him killed.

"Ready?" She led the way to the garage door through the kitchen, marching by the dynamic duo, who were still busy honing their fighting skills on one another.

He shook his head, but couldn't help hold back a smile at the adorable kittens trying to appear vicious and mean to each other, yowling and spitting in an endeavor to be alpha kitty. It had been a long time since he had had the luxury of downtime to watch kittens play. *A lifetime ago.* His spirits bolstered, he moved after Lily. He found himself eager to check out the land and learn more about this independent woman with the marshmallow heart who took in wounded animals and people, mending them back to health. Still cautious and hesitant, he couldn't dampen the urge to prod into Lily's life, learn more, and declare her a rough, rare yellow diamond or a typical self-centered female, well-practiced in deceit.

Just the negative words in the same sentence as her name rang untrue. He held to that hope and prepared for the worst. A practice he'd excelled at over the years.

Gray clouds covered the sun, leaving the morning chilly, damp, and dreary. Pulling his collar up, Cale stepped into the biting wind. His insulated jacket with multiple layers could handle this weather without a problem. Sliding a glance to his right, he considered Lily and her threadbare coat. Surely she had something better and warmer to wear? It could barely work for today, but deep in winter, Jack Frost could easily blow right through it like a breeze through a screen door.

She's not my responsibility. He would be gone in a few days, anyway. *So why bother?*

The reminder soured his optimism.

Cale raked the terrain, searching for dangers, obstacles, hidden venues, and signs that someone had somehow followed them to this isolated spot on the map. The fresh air cleared his lungs, with the scent of hay and livestock spurring memories from eons ago. Good memories that he'd tucked away when he needed to remember some happiness existed in life.

Just inside the fence tilled dirt lay bare, probably in preparation for next year's garden. He could see her on hands and knees planting and nurturing the seeds to grow, collecting the harvest, and preserving it for winter meals.

Lily pulled up on the water pump, letting water flow quickly into the large round metal water trough. Her eyebrows furrowed as she used a finger to count cows standing around a small barn that sat a couple of hundred feet away, with the doors pulled open. A half-eaten round bale sat nearby with three cows slowly eating off it while others rested in the litter it created.

"All here and accounted for?" Cale asked, noting the large boned, white to cream colored cattle. Muscles and sheer size impressed him, especially the herd bull. In addition to the extra bulk, a rounded hump sat just in front of his shoulders. These weren't just average run-of-the-mill livestock. Unless he missed his guess, these were expensive beef cattle bred for the show ring as much as anything.

"Yep. All twenty-five." She smiled, turned off the water, and ushered Cale through the small gate located to the right of the water pump, allowing them entrance into the field.

He glanced warily at the bull moving toward them, one hand automatically reaching for the handgun he carried in his shoulder vest under his jacket. He stepped forward to place himself in the animal's path, only for Lily to walk around him, out to meet the trotting mammoth.

"Good morning, Hard Head." She cooed to the bull, scratching his forehead and around his ears. The bull lowered his head and leaned into the caress, obviously used to and enjoying the fussing.

Cale shook his head and relaxed his stance. *A pet.* Leave it to Lily to befriend such a creature. "Hard Head?" His lips twitched at the name.

Lily continued her ministrations while glancing his direction. "Well, that's not his registered name, of course. But, it's an appropriate nickname for this guy." She giggled when, just like one of her cats, the bull rested his head against her belly, begging for more attention. Dutifully scratching, she talked to the bull, showering him with affection.

He would have sworn old Hard Head groaned in pleasure as her quick fingers rubbed over a particularly itchy spot. *Just like I would if those same hands caressed me, stroking and molding to my body while she whispered words of endearment, praise, and longing. She would lean over, her shoulder-length blonde hair brushing over my erection before those teasing hazel eyes sparkled in mischief as her tongue reached out to sample from the liquid forming at the tip.*

"I'm going to walk the fence line." Lily started toward the metal barrier.

Cale yanked hard on the reins of his control. What was wrong with him? He was acting like a frisky teenager with his first taste of passion. Shifting, Cale bit back the discomfort from his body's natural reactions to the stark images in his mind. One day with this woman and he was already imagining things he had no business even daydreaming about. Hadn't he learned his lesson well enough before?

With Lily, he wasn't sure one night would be long enough.

Muttering a curse, he set out after her.

And when the hell did she slip under his guard? He chastised himself for pronouncing her sweet, harmless, and in need of a good man to teach her about the birds and bees. Yet, as hard as he tried to resurrect that brick wall around himself, he couldn't quite manage the task. Something about Lily called to him, reached inside and plucked at his long lost sense of humor. Fear of her ease at getting through his carefully constructed barriers would put him totally on the defensive if she didn't ring true with each and every word and action. She might be lying, but she'd be the world's best at doing so. He'd met his fair share, learned to detect untruths by many means after leaving his betraying wife, and vowed never to be taken in again.

Not ready to throw in the towel, he cautioned himself to proceed slowly before giving her a free pass. After all, more than one man died with a look of surprise on his face.

His long strides allowed him to quickly catch up as she walked north along the fence line. The echoes of cattle rustling and picking at late season grass along with the calls of a crow looking for breakfast were the only sounds he detected. In truth, the quietness of nature calmed him and eased the tension that had ridden him hard since Dillon had taken the bullet. One could easily forget the world's problems, let their life slow down, and soak up the tranquility offered by the rural setting. Nature at its best.

They ambled in companionable silence for a while, making their way around the several acres of pasture, checking the barbed wire fence for breaks or damage as they progressed.

Cale broke the silence. "No calves?"

She shook her head. "Carson doesn't want fall calves owing to the hard winter. Oh, they would probably be fine as much as he and Cody take care of them, but he'd rather just play it safe with spring babies."

"Cody?"

"He's Carson's herd caretaker, for lack of a better word. Very nice guy. Hard-working and really cares about the animals. He'd give you the shirt off his back if he thought you needed it." She paused to tug at a fence post, moving forward when it didn't give.

He tried to read between the lines with her statements about Cody. If they were a couple, he couldn't tell by the inflection in her voice. Instinct told him she had no man, at least at the present time. The knowledge soothed his surprising possessive tendencies surrounding the little nurse.

"You should see the babies in the spring—crisp white and cream colored, bellowing, butting heads, bouncing around the pasture. I could watch their antics for hours, just forgetting the world existed besides this little corner of paradise." Her face glowed with a bright smile.

Cale's breath caught at the sheer joy he saw in her expression. Not many women would be trudging out in the cold, walking along a fence, and blatantly happy with the thought of sitting in the grass mesmerized by calves at play. His heart tugged once more. *Time for a subject change.* "You aren't from here?"

"No." Her happiness fled with his question, bringing a more somber tone. "After Mother passed, all I had left were memories and loneliness. I decided I needed a new start in life with a new location, job, everything."

"A new man?" He could have kicked himself when the question slipped out. Instead, he watched her body language closely, seeking truth in her words.

She paused, sending him a look of puzzlement. "I didn't have a man then or now, if you must know." A subtle bite of annoyance laced her voice.

Changing directions in the conversation, he pressed for more information. "What will you do after this?"

Lily rotated, now following the fence as it headed to the farthest corner of the vast pasture. "Cajole your brother into taking a bath to help clean out his wound. Hang more antibiotics. Dust, mop the floors. Get the turkey out of the freezer to thaw. Make that pie and feed the bottomless pits again."

He couldn't bite back the small grin. Leave it to her to take the question literally. "Actually, I meant life plans, like job, home, and family. And I'll get my brother into the bath."

"You'll cajole him, huh?" She smiled widely up at him, batting her lashes in play.

"No cajoling about it. I'll toss his ass in if he doesn't cooperate." Enjoying her teasing, he reached out to tug on a tuft of hair blowing in the stout breeze. "Now, back to those future plans?"

She shook her head, but didn't hesitate to answer. "No plans, really. As far as I know, I'm staying here."

"You never want to move or change careers?" He pressed for more.

"Nope. Right now I'm happy. Content. I enjoy my job and truly feel almost peaceful where I'm at. Who could ask for anything more?"

Who could? Lots of women probably would fit in that category, wanting to take a relatively easy role in life and let their man take care of them. Fine if that's what worked for a couple. However, he avoided those types like the plague. Been there, done that once and never again.

"How about you? Got a man in your life?"

The phrasing caught him off guard, breaking his normally graceful stride to a near stumble. It took a second for him to realize her brand of bantering. He snorted loudly. "As if."

"Okay. What about a woman in your life?"

Even though he realized the natural progression of the conversation would lead to that very inquiry, he flinched hearing it voiced. Jaw clenching, he clammed up, not willing to discuss such a hurtful period of his life.

* * * *

Lily shut her mouth, seeing the heart-wrenching pain appear for a split second on Cale's face in response to her question. If she hadn't been watching him so closely at the time, she would have missed the telltale cringe. He seemed to be relaxing and possibly even enjoying their walk and discussion until she had to ask about his prior relationships. Sure, most people had them and wore a few badges of courage to show for their efforts, but not often did she see such torment on a person's face with a simple mention of the opposite sex. Guilt rose up inside, sending her gaze to the ground. *What horrors must he have suffered to react so negatively?* Quickly, she kicked her mind into motion, seeking something else to say, anything to put back the handsome smile he had flashed earlier. "You said you have parents?"

He only nodded in response.

Charging ahead, she tossed out the first response that came to mind. "Good to know. Here I was ready to strip you and Dillon down to check for belly buttons. I feared there would be none and then what would I do? Who do you call when you find a belly button-less person? And if there is no belly button, where does all that lint go to hide?" Holding her breath, she waited a tick, watching intently, hoping she cracked his stony façade once more.

Cale's bottom lip twitched in the slightest motion.

Taking that as positive, she rambled on. "I can just hear the phone call now. Bureau of Alien Life, how can I help you? Yes, ma'am, I need to report two men without belly buttons. What do they look like? Well, tall, dark, and handsome, minus belly buttons. What do you mean that isn't your department? Whose department is it? Oh, then can you transfer me? Hello? Department of the Interior, I need to report men without navels. Huh? What navy? No. No. Without navels. You know. Belly button. What? I've already talked to the Bureau of Alien Life, they sent me to you. Wait. I don't think that's the correct department that I need. Well, drat. Hello, is this the Department of the Mentally Deranged? Well, you see. I need to report navel-less men. Yes. As in no belly buttons. What do you mean do I hallucinate often?"

Cale burst out laughing, the sound literally music to Lily's ears. "You're right about the government."

She had thought him handsome before, but the addition of humor added a glorious glow and softened his normally stern expression, which only added to his overall gorgeous status. Lily smiled with satisfaction and pride. *He needs to laugh more.* If it took silliness to get this present day warrior to laugh, then so be it. She was up to the task.

Not that she had much experience with men, but this one captivated her. She knew nothing about him or his brother, yet had begrudgingly allowed strangers into her home. Now, she dedicated herself to helping this way too serious guy to find amusement in his life again. *Maybe I should be talking to the Department of the Mentally Deranged after all.*

One look at Cale and her heart fluttered. He stood a head taller, muscular and toned, strong and sound. He probably could have been a male model if he had so desired. No. That didn't seem to quite fit. His features were stark and sharp, beautiful in a rough, primitive way. Those light blue eyes reflected an inner demon, but flashed with mischief now and again, hinting at a deeply buried sense of playfulness. Something she desperately wanted to stoke.

The man is out of your league. Her inner voice reminded her that she didn't stand a chance with the soldier. He'd move on in a few days, never once looking back or thinking about her. With his bold looks and strong nature, he would have the pick of the henhouse. She, on the other hand, would be outside in the trees, roosting with the less desirable females. Mentally, she shrugged. She liked him, and perhaps, with time and fate, it could progress into something more than a simple houseguest and nurse, but she dared not buy into those dreams. Even if he noticed her, he would kiss her, then dash away to save the world.

Is it better to have loved and lost than to never have loved at all? It wouldn't be love on his part anyway. From what she could faintly see from his demeanor, he didn't believe in love. She would be a physical release, nothing more.

Forcefully, she pushed that sobering thought aside. *There I go again putting the cart before the horse.* One day at a time. One smile at a time. This she would do. *For him.*

Chapter Eight

Dillon automatically tensed when the door creaked, announcing someone's arrival into the house. Before he could place his hand on the handgun stashed under his pillow, Cale's familiar voice carried to him. Relaxing back into the soft mattress, he resumed lightly stroking the soft fur on the cats.

He'd awoken a few minutes before with both kittens curled against his side. Hope climbed to settle in the middle of his chest, turning circles until she found a comfortable position to plop down. Normally he woke with the slightest touch or noise, yet they had snuggled in without him having a clue. A bit worrying, but he immediately waved off the concern when all three began to purr, responding to his petting.

Cale stuck his head in the bedroom door, taking in the sight, a slow grin forming on his face.

"What?"

Leaning against the doorjamb with arms crossed over his chest, Cale shook his head. "Found some new bedmates?"

Dillon snorted. "At least they don't hog the covers and snore like a chainsaw trying to cut through granite like you do."

"Uh-huh."

Lily popped her head around Cale, smiling immediately at the sight. "Oh, they like you."

Barely resisting the urge to roll his eyes, Dillon nodded. "I guess so. But I really think they just want to be scratched and have a warm body to snuggle against."

"Nah. They wouldn't be all over you unless they liked you."

Dillon shot his brother a mischievous grin. "Well, I always did have a way with the ladies."

Cale's lips moved, but Lily talked over him. "Carson wanted you to sit in the bathtub for a while each day. It will help clean out that wound and prevent infection from building." Lily rattled the recommendations to Dillon while she lifted the girls, cradling them against her chest. They made for an overloaded armful.

"Okay. I think I can do that." He grinned at her, unable to pass up the opportunity to tease. "You can wash my back...and whatever else you like." Purposely, he dropped to a sensual tone, not so subtly covering the innuendo.

Cale scowled at him from behind her back, but Dillon ignored him, too thrilled to get his older brother's goat for once.

Her face flushed crimson, amusing him all the more before she shook her head. "Sorry. I can't take the chance. See, if I discover you really don't have a belly button... Well, let's just say it's easier if I don't know." She shot him a quick wink and grin before striding out of the room with a hasty excuse that it was feeding time for the felines.

Dillon watched her go in abject confusion. *Belly button?* "What in the hell did that mean?"

Cale grinned widely, slapping Dillon on the shoulder. "You really don't want to know."

Lily's voice carried to them from the kitchen. "Are you cajoling?"

Even more confused than ever, Dillon looked to Cale for answers. "Cajoling?"

"Yeah. I'm supposed to 'cajole' you into taking a bath."

His mouth dropped open. Never in his wildest dreams would he have expected to hear those words leave Cale's mouth.

"Don't worry. I assured her I'd simply drop you on your ass in the tub."

"Thank God. For a second there I wondered if you lost your ever-loving mind."

The sound of Cale's chuckle rang through the room. Dillon joined in, his heart lifting with the sudden reappearance of Cale's sense of humor. Not too long ago, he'd believed the feat to be impossible. This was his brother of old. The one he loved and longed to reacquaint himself with.

Lily reminded him of Della. Her attitude toward life, the old soul he could see in her eyes, and the deep down kindness so rare to find these days. Cale could do a lot worse. He had already done so, in Dillon's opinion.

His thoughts returned to Rachel, Cale's ex-wife. Never would she have taken in an injured and ill cat, nursed it back to health, and adamantly refused to give up the resulting kittens. No way would Rachel spend her little excess money on pricey cat food, give them the run of the house, and allow them to sleep curled up next to her at night. On the contrary, Cale's ex disliked all animals with a passion. Her few run-ins resulted in multiple complaints about the animals slobbering, getting hair on her expensive designer clothes, and the horrible stench she believed they carried. The couple of times Cale had brought her home to the ranch, she had sulked and moaned, demanding to leave as soon as possible, more than ready to return to her high-class apartment in the city. Their parents had frowned on the woman, as had Dillon. Yet no one could make Cale see her multiple faults and using ways. Not until he finally woke up one day, when reality slapped him in the face. Hard.

Dillon had been with him that day, returning home after finishing their mission quickly, efficiently, and much sooner than expected. Excited to get home to Rachel, Cale drove straight for the apartment, full of plans to take her out on the town, and romance her mightily to make up for the days he'd been away.

Instead of a doting wife, missing her husband, and joyous at his return, Cale had found Rachel sharing their bed with another man, naked, and in mid-fuck. The man had grabbed his clothes after taking one look at Cale's face, scurrying away as quickly as possible.

Rachel had caught the brunt of Cale's fury, but instead of being apologetic, had flung it back in his face, citing her reasons for placing the blame fully on Cale. He wasn't home enough. He didn't have enough money. He didn't please her. On and on she went.

Dillon had never seen his brother so angry and so devastated. Without uttering another word, Cale had turned around and left, filing for divorce the very next morning. A difficult way to have his eyes opened about the true bitch he married. Effective but painful.

Yet a day with Lily, and Cale's sense of humor returned at least partially, as his chuckles, teasing manner, and smile indicated. Still too brief in Dillon's opinion, but they were there — a sure sign of hope. Lily did that. He would be forever beholden to her for bringing a bit of life back into the robotic, emotionless brother he'd seen for the past two years.

Dillon couldn't begin to guess what Cale and Lily had spoken about on their tour of the field, but he saw a more relaxed Cale, one who seemingly gave Lily his nod of approval.

Interesting and right on track with Dillon's own plans.

Chapter Nine

Lily clunked the solidly frozen turkey into the kitchen sink, breathing deeply with the effort to lug the heavy bird in from the garage freezer. "Now, where are the instructions that tell me how to cook this thing?" she muttered to herself, twirling it around until she spied a white plastic label.

"Why go to the trouble to bake a whole turkey?" Cale asked from his seat at the table while he and Dillon finished their lunch. "That's too much work. Besides, we'll be gone soon anyway."

Her heart sank—hearing those words reminded her that only too soon her roommates would be running off, back to the line of fire, not knowing if they would live one day to the next. The wonderful plans for Thanksgiving she'd concocted now looked frivolous and foolish. She could've kicked herself for not mentioning her idea sooner. Perhaps they might have been more receptive then. *Too late now.* She turned to face them, her gaze focusing on the table instead of their faces. "I'm sorry. I didn't even think to ask. I just thought... Well, Thanksgiving is two days away, and… I thought we might celebrate it together." The final words were blurted out. Glancing up, she noted the scowl that Dillon aimed at Cale.

Cale shook his head, but finally released a deep sigh, seeming to give in to the silent pressure. He stood. He gently raised her chin with one long index finger until she met his eyes. "If you're sure, we'd like to share the holiday with you."

She breathed out a sigh of happiness and relief then grinned.

Cale's finger turned into a small caress across her jaw until he lightly tapped her nose. "But you have to let us help."

"Deal." With a heavy weight lifted off her shoulders, she mouthed a quick 'thanks' to Dillon, before regarding Cale again.

He stroked across her cheek once more, cradling it for a split second before letting his hand fall back to his side. Light blue eyes smiled back. "Dillon is great at washing dishes."

"Hey!" Dillon hollered from the table, reaching for his crutches to hold at a threatening angle, as if to smack Cale over the head.

"You don't know how much this means to me," Lily confessed, her voice wobbling with emotion.

"I think we do." Dillon's voice carried across the room, solid and reassuring.

Her confidant in battle. The battle for Cale's humanity.

She looked at Dillon, belatedly noticing the drastic improvement food, rest, and basic medical care had made in him, both mentally and physically.

After an early morning phone call for a status update, Carson had her stop the IV fluids since he didn't think Dillon needed them as his appetite had picked up right where it left off. He would be able to care for his own hydration needs without assistance. The IV itself remained, giving her access to the antibiotics he still required. But the extra freedom proved beneficiary to Dillon's mobility and mood. While still slow, he maneuvered much better with the crutches, more confident and secure. Cale didn't have to step in at all since that first time. Give Dillon another day or so and he might outrun them both.

Tears sprang up in her eyes, but she dashed them away. Never would she have dreamed how much she wanted and needed them to be with her. This was the first major holiday since her mother passed, and as much as she told herself it was just another day, it simply wasn't. If they hadn't been there, she would have buried herself in work, anything to avoid thinking and remembering for fear of spending hours crying once more for her loss. Her closets might shine from cleaning and organizing along with freshly waxed floors, but she would've been hard-pressed to not recall happier times and feel the heart-wrenching pain all over again. "Thank you. Really." With a sniff, she beamed at Cale.

Although she'd known them less than forty-eight hours and they hadn't uttered a single deep dark secret about who they really were and why one of them had shown up with a bullet to the leg, she went with her gut. They'd had more than enough time to rob her, kill her, and dash off with her hand-me-down couch full of lumps. They had been good company. Although Cale had started out surly, he'd thawed enough to make her see him in a brand new light, one full of sexual promise and desire. She shoved the thought from her mind, unwilling to linger too long on the risqué thoughts for fear she might open her mouth and the words slip out unheeded.

His eyes shadowed for a second before rubbing her upper arm. "Don't thank us yet."

"Yeah, well. Don't thank me yet either. I've never cooked a full turkey before, and I hear the first time is painful and unfulfilling. Too dry or some such matter."

Cale snorted. Dillon coughed.

It took her a moment to realize where their minds had ventured with her phrasing—straight down to the gutter. Heat blasted across her face.

Bright white teeth flashed as Cale smiled at her. "It's all in the preparation." The low husky tone left her certain he wasn't talking about the turkey.

Good grief. Kicking her hamster wheel of a brain into gear, Lily valiantly tried to find a new topic, anything besides the not so subtle reference to her virginity. Granted, the guys didn't know such intimate details about her and she preferred to keep it that way. But the direction of this conversation landed way too close for her comfort.

It wasn't that she didn't want a boyfriend or was one of those that swore to abstain from sex until marriage. Instead, it was something more practical. Life happened, sex didn't. The few dates she'd been on had been okay, but she'd never felt at ease enough with the guy to do more than a few kisses and touches. None of them had inspired her to get naked and do the horizontal mambo.

Not the way Cale did.

She immediately threw the idea away. As he'd said before, they would leave soon. Even if he took her to his bed...well, make that *her* bed...it would last for an impossibly short duration before he rode off into the sunset, leaving her lonely and brokenhearted.

But he called to her. His moodiness, the troubled past she read in his eyes, his dangerous career and potentially shortened life. Everything about him pulled her closer, like a hungry and stressed woman to a chocolate store as reckless and destined for failure as it might be. She wanted to soothe him, care for him, and share laughs and each day's small miracles with him. Here stood a man she could love, if only she let herself.

I've only known him for a day! The chastisement meant nothing to her heart. Normally, she mocked the idea of love at first sight. Now, she couldn't be so sure. But so much rested on his shoulders. *Why would he be interested in me? Even want to sleep with me? Pity? Or as a basic show of appreciation for what I did?*

His rough hand rested against her cheek, distracting her from such sobering thoughts. "Where did you go?" Cale asked, tilting his head

Lily peeked over to find that Dillon had quietly left the kitchen under his own power, heading easily to the family room, leaving them in a semblance of privacy.

"Oh, nowhere. It's...nothing," she stammered, refusing to lie, but determined to not voice her innermost feelings to him.

He stared at her a bit longer, gaze roaming her face before he slowly leaned in. Reflexively, she closed her eyes, waited with anticipation, then felt his soft lips gently settle over hers. No aggressiveness or demands existed, simply a sharing of affection between two people. He flicked his tongue along the seam, then sucked on her upper lip in a tender display. Her heart sang as shivers of excitement shot through her veins.

A mere meeting of lips and she wanted more. Needed more.

He stepped back, adjusted his stance to wrap his arms around her waist, and tugged her closer as his lips once more settled over hers. Eagerly, she offered up her mouth to his.

"Ow!" Cale yanked back to growl. Charity—claws extended, perched halfway up his pant legs on her way to higher ground—was climbing him like she would a tree.

Lily blinked at the sudden interruption, reaching out to grab the kitten before she could draw more blood. "Bad Charity."

Cale shook his head, rubbing his thigh before peering down at the small white and orange spotted fur ball in her arms. "Give a guy a warning next time." He spoiled the chastisement with a tender rubbing of Charity's head. Glancing up, he met Lily's gaze.

She smiled shyly, holding and stroking the smaller of the two kittens. His kiss had been exceptional and way too short. She knew the memory would last throughout the day and then some. Who knew such a hard man could possess such tenderness?

The expression on his face sent her belly to flip-flopping with longing. He moved forward once more, brushing his mouth over hers for a mere fleeting second before speaking. "I think she's hungry." He scanned the area before drawing back to Charity. "You're the messenger, huh?"

The kitten meowed demandingly, then stared up at him intently with her big blue eyes.

Cale chuckled at her, petting her head, before setting her down with the rest of the small family. "Yeah, yeah. We get it."

Lily glimpsed down to see Hope and Faith sitting at the empty food platters, looking up at them pitifully. She couldn't help but grin. A few seconds later, she popped the top off a couple of cans of food, filled the bowls, and returned to Cale's side.

They stood in silence, watching and listening to the cats gulp down their favorite meal with relish and enjoyment. She leaned her smaller frame against his side, thrilled when he wrapped an arm around her, holding her close.

Her heart lifted as she enjoyed another day's small miracle. Mother and babies that shouldn't have survived, all scarfing down food despite their already plump bellies. And a man who had lost the ability to feel happiness smiling openly at the scene before him.

Chapter Ten

Cale strode out of the back door, intending to make one more sweep of the area before dinner. He couldn't rule out Lansing's mob tailing them from their latest mission, the one that had left Dillon wounded but alive. The same wasn't true for two of the men they sought. If their information proved correct, three more survived simply because they weren't where they were supposed to be that night. It made for a dangerous and often shitty outcome. Half-done got him and his team killed. Lansing wasn't the kind of man to let bygones be bygones. Best he could figure, their hasty travel bought them time, perhaps a couple of days or more. But Lansing would come gunning for them, and soon. Before then, Dillon needed to recover more. Cale also had to find a way to protect Lily on the off-chance someone linked her with them. Nothing stood in the way of what that bastard wanted. *Fodder.* Lansing considered them cannon fodder.

Shaking his head to push out those morbid thoughts, he surveyed the pastures. Cattle rested and chewed their cud, content as if they hadn't a worry in the world. Who knew what a cow thought, but these particular ones probably didn't have many stressors. Food, water, shelter, and several lady friends for Hard Head. A simple life. For a cow.

After lunch, Cale had hauled his brother into the bath for another soaking of that wound, while Lily had cleaned the kitchen and set food out for the dinner she planned to fix later. Then she'd taken a quick shower, finishing in plenty of time to re-dress Dillon's leg and attach another antibiotic to his IV. She'd barely eaten any lunch, citing not being hungry, even as both he and Dillon had cleaned their plates, appreciative of the fresh, hot meal. Her gaze kept darting to him as if she recalled what had occurred and now wasn't sure how she felt about their interaction.

His thoughts meandered back to Lily and the chaste kiss they'd shared earlier. Whatever had possessed him to seal his lips over hers, to get a small taste of her essence? Truth be told, the shadowed, hollow sadness in her eyes had twisted something deep in his gut, especially when his flippant words had caused such pain. It moved him to offer comfort in a small gesture that felt right. *Boy, did it feel right.* He couldn't claim naivety, and over the years had kissed more women than he cared to recall. However, this one touched a part of him he'd thought dead and gone when he'd walked in and found his wife with another man. Lily made him want to care again, to laugh at her silliness, and to spend that all-important Thanksgiving dinner with her for no other reason than it would make them both happy.

She was different from other women he had been with. More pure. Fairly innocent, too, if he didn't miss his guess. In his world, that was as rare as a blue diamond laying in the middle of a pasture. But it was more than that. *Down to earth and common as the day was long.* One of his father's favorite phrases popped into his head. Lily could fit the bill. Heck, his parents would adore her.

What in the hell am I thinking? Introducing her to his parents? That meant a long-term relationship. Something he'd vowed to never enter into again. Betrayal was an excellent teacher. Hell, if she was as innocent as he thought, he really should keep his hands to himself. No sense in leading her on, sleeping with her, then riding off to his next assignment, leaving her like an astronaut left the earth with the possibility of never returning. Lily deserved better—a committed husband to stand beside her and together raise a family. To give her the simple farm life she longed for.

He couldn't be that man. *Wouldn't* be that man. His life revolved around the Wind Warriors, fighting the baddest of the bad behind the scenes and in the dark. Only a handful of people knowing of their existence. Men he would give his life for, as they would for him. They thrived on adrenaline and challenge, constant change and seclusion. That was his career and sole focus now and would continue to be.

Wives and children were a cherished novelty and as uncommon as a flood in the Sahara Desert. Their work, though necessary, often claimed their lives and their sanity. Hardened veterans, they saw and lived through too many waking nightmares for any of them to retire to polite society. A normal job would never do for any of them.

All former military, they could return to those ranks if they were desperate enough and decided to swallow their independence and abilities in order to be puppets to whichever commander they would be stuck under. But in Wind Warriors they could excel, having the clearance to do what they thought best with no questions asked. A flexibility that most men craved, a paycheck to compensate for all the inconveniences and hazard pay, along with access to all the newest and greatest weapons produced across the world.

What else could a man ask for?

Lily.

The kind of woman a man would give anything to come home to, stand in her arms, and soak up all the love and comfort she could provide. To spend the rest of their lives knowing that love did exist and they could share decades of exploring that love, reveling in it, and passing it on for future generations to be a part of.

The woman he couldn't have and the dream that couldn't come true. Reality told him this, yet his mind grasped for possibilities, tormented him with the magical 'what if' questions, giving him fleeting glimpses of a haunting paradise.

Until someone took a bite of that damned apple.

He shook his head at the analogy.

Most likely, he'd leave behind a grieving girlfriend before they could reach a single anniversary owing to the risks of his job. If a bullet didn't find him, something else might. No lack of danger existed in his day-to-day life. Something he wasn't ready to share with an innocent like Lily.

How could she be so trusting, so believing, so sweet? Opening her doors to him and Dillon based on a recommendation from her boss. Didn't she know the world was full of hardened criminals just waiting to prey on the inner goodness of others?

His protective streak flared. He owed Lily and would keep the wolves away from her door. All of them. No one would harm her. He'd tear their damn head off first.

Whoa.

The intensity of the promise startled him as little else could—forcing him to see the naked truth. Somehow, Lily had slipped past his guard in record time, dug deep, and made herself at home. The realization didn't settle comfortably.

Didn't I learn anything from that fiasco called a marriage?

With a heavy sigh, Cale trudged toward the house, filled with contradiction and indecision. No matter how much he lectured himself, he couldn't find an answer for the woman who stuck in his head like superglue.

Chapter Eleven

Stepping back into the house, Cale sniffed deeply, drawing in the scents of simmering stew and cornbread, along with a freshly baked blueberry pie, which sat on the countertop cooling. In the background, the washer and dryer cleaned clothes while the dishwasher hummed, polishing the dirty dishes from earlier meals. His stomach growled at the enticing aromas while something near his heart clenched in a sure feeling of rightness.

A man could get used to this. He certainly could. After years of survival on the run, coming home to dinner and a warm woman who loved him would be more than a dream. It would be paradise.

He shook off those thoughts, still grappling with scarred emotions from a harsh, but effective lesson. Glancing around, he found Lily. She sat on the couch, holding a stick with a piece of material attached, making it jump and dance as the kittens leaped and grabbed in obvious delight. He grinned, not just from the amusement of watching the babies, but at seeing Lily finally relaxing. The girl had more energy than a small terrier and spent most of the time on one chore or another, from what he'd seen thus far. No doubt about it. She worked hard.

"Where's Dillon?"

She looked up from her task. "On the phone with Della."

Anger shot to the fore along with a hefty burst of trepidation. Dillon knew better. No communication rules during a job existed for a reason. The men they sought weren't dumb or ignorant. They could easily pick up a cell phone tracer on any of their lines and follow them to the source, either to the Wind Warrior himself or to the person they spoke with. Frowning, he turned toward the bedroom, prepared to read his brother the riot act for putting them as well as his girlfriend in absolute danger.

Lily's face morphed from happy greeting to bafflement before something obviously clicked in her mind. "He's using my cell phone. I offered. After all, she would want to know he's okay. I would if I were in her shoes."

Cale's attention snapped back to her, his mouth falling open before he shut it again. His moment of temper vanished as he processed the new information. They should be safe using Lily's phone. Dillon hadn't taken advantage and asked. Thus, he could only chalk it up to Lily's kindness and ability to read beneath the surface. A potentially deadly skill if she didn't possess the goodness he saw in her over and over again. With a sigh, he relaxed onto the couch beside her, absently stroking Hope when she climbed on his lap, purring loudly.

"Please don't be mad at him. It was my suggestion and offer. I thought it might help him feel better and recover faster, getting to at least talk with the woman he loves." Lily bobbed the stick again. Charity grabbed the end of the cloth with teeth and claws, refusing to let go of her prize. Faith batted at her until Lily found a toy mouse, tossing it near the black and white spotted kitten, watching her smack it and chase it around on the hardwood floor.

He couldn't argue with that logic. "It's okay. And, I think you're right. It'll do him good to talk to her."

Lily continued to watch the babies. "He told me she's an elementary school teacher."

Cale nodded, not really surprised Dillon had spoken of Della to Lily. She had a talent for charming things out of a guy. Look how much they'd shared with her in just over a day. Not an awful lot to some, but a generous amount in their line of business.

"They hope to marry soon. Settle down. Raise a family."

"Yeah." He knew all that a while back.

"You don't approve?" Lily glanced up.

He shrugged. "I like Della. She's a good woman who I think can make Dillon happy. I really wish them the best."

"But…"

He waited until Hope turned a couple of rounds before settling comfortably in his lap, tucking her front paws under and closing her eyes. "I worry what kind of job Dillon will find. It's not like he can mesh back into polite society easily. He needs excitement and a challenge. We all do."

"We?"

Debating on how to answer that question, Cale took a long breath. "We—others who do the same kind of job. It's not nine to five, no holidays, no weekends. It's a go from the moment the phone rings until the job is done. Then you regroup and head off to the next one."

She nodded. "What exactly is it you do?" Lily whispered as if she'd considered not speaking then at all.

He debated for a moment then went with his gut. "We're a small group of men who are paid to ferret out particularly nasty criminals and capture them." Send them to hell was more like it. But he didn't want her expression of interest and trust to turn into one of disgust and repulsion. No. He needed her acceptance, her continued interest, the look of mindfulness of his maleness when she thought he didn't notice. Once he had received those precious gifts, he stubbornly refused to return them, holding them protectively like a child with a favored Christmas present. Cale watched her features closely, as his words soaked in.

She reached over, twining her smaller fingers with his. Softness descended over her face. "Unfortunately, someone has to do it. If you didn't, I fear the world would become a darker and more treacherous place."

His shoulders slumped in relief at her quick approval.

"I can only imagine the dangers you and Dillon must face. It has to be doubly hard on Della." She looked down, whispering beneath her breath, "I'll worry about you, too."

He cupped her cheek, turning her head until her eyes met his. After leaning in, he brought their lips together, seeking the pleasure and sweetness he'd savored once before. She returned his attentions, sending fire directly from his mind down to his groin. With a low moan, he opened her mouth with his own, slipping his tongue in for a deeper taste.

Lily drew a ragged breath, but allowed his explorations, giving back as she shyly moved to run her tongue across his.

That simple action spurred his libido. He tugged her closer with an arm around her waist, as he reclaimed control of the kiss, pushing for greater depth, starving for another sample of delicious essence that belonged solely to Lily. *Ambrosia.* Her tentative responses reminded him to focus on slow and steady even as they heated his blood to a frenzied state. She could burn him to a pile of ashes at this rate. If her kiss was this hot, what would it be like to lay her down on the king-sized bed, spread out for him to see and appreciate? His engorged cock would spear inside, separating those glorious, glistening, pink folds on his way to the promised land.

"Earth to Cale."

Dillon's voice broke into his erotic daydream.

Lily pulled back, face flushed from passion or embarrassment, or a mixture of both. Cale hoped it was the former.

Tearing his gaze from Lily, he glanced at his brother. Dillon stood behind the couch with what could only be called a shit-eating grin on his face — so much for keeping his feelings for their hostess under wraps. "Don't you have someone else to bedevil?"

Dillon chuckled deeply, looking first at Cale then to Lily before returning once again. "Nope."

Cale snorted, shifting to ease the tightness below.

"If you will excuse me, dinner should be done." With that said, Lily retreated.

Cale glared at his younger brother, frustrated with the inopportune interruption. "What is it?"

"I thought the poor girl needed to come up for air." Dillon's wicked grin told the real story.

Dillon would never pass up a chance to give him a hard time. A younger brother's prerogative, he claimed. However, he was going to kick Dillon's ass for interrupting them and sending Lily scurrying off like a wild filly at the first glimpse of a cowboy with a saddle.

"I think you must like her." Dillon's whisper carried to Cale's ears.

Not liking the topic of conversation, Cale ignored him until Dillon plopped down beside him and elbowed him hard in the gut. His low growl didn't deter the kid, either.

"She's a good woman. Reminds me of Della. Someone a man can come home to, who'll be there for him, and love him to pieces."

"We're leaving after Thanksgiving." The tone brooked no argument.

Dillon grinned. "Then you better get in gear, big bro. Not much time to make that pretty girl yours."

A scowl formed on Cale's face. "I...can't."

"Can't or won't?"

"We're leaving...soon. She doesn't deserve to be left brokenhearted with no hope of a relationship. She needs a man who'll come home every night, shower her with kisses, and hold her through the long cold nights." His own words sank deep, hitting him like a punch to the gut. *Damn it. It's true. I want to be that man.* "She needs more than what I can offer. A life on the run with no rest or safety. That's no way to raise a family."

"Why not you?" Dillon questioned again.

Throwing his arms up in frustration, Cale faced his brother, barely noticing when Hope jumped down, obviously uncomfortable with his jerky motions. "Have you forgotten what we do? How dangerous it is? Not only for us, but for anyone linked to us? How can I play with her emotions, run off, leaving her alone and unprotected, while I do my job, perhaps never seeing her again?"

Dillon's lips compressed once more. "You don't think I've considered each and every one of those arguments before? Believing that Della would be better off finding another man with a more stable lifestyle? Let me tell you something she told me that makes a hell of a lot of sense. None of us know how much time we have on earth. She would much rather be with the man she loves, for however long she gets, than to go through life wishing for something that could have been. Della is strong. So is Lily. They understand and will face fire to be with the men they love."

Cale savored those words for a long moment, considering the message being pounded into his head. With a sigh, he laid his head back on the couch, running one large hand through his short hair. "I can't bear to see anything happen to her. Not to mention Lansing is still out there." Still whispered, the words carried more emotion than he would have preferred. He had barely admitted the same to himself, after all, let alone babble the facts to others. Including Dillon.

Dillon slapped him on the shoulder in an age-old sign of support. "I know." He paused for a beat before continuing. "I'm considering retiring."

He stared at his brother in shock. "Really? Since when?"

"Since I've been serious with Della. It's true she'll accept whatever decision I make on the job, but I want more for her."

"So, she's talked you into quitting?" Cale frowned at the thought.

Dillon shook his head. "No. I haven't even mentioned it to her yet. It was just an idea, considering my future. Our future. Truth is, I want to be there with her, come home to her smiling face, spend the nights cuddled up instead of freezing my ass off in the mountains, lying in a snow bank, and waiting out a hit."

Cale nodded. "I've briefly thought about it, too. But what other job is there to do for us? We aren't cut out to work nine to five, sitting on our asses in a cubicle."

"I'm not sure, but I've been giving it some thought. Perhaps there's something in the organization without being on the front lines or with another agency. Heck, even being a local cop is possible. I just need to do a bit of research, but I know there has to be something. Other men have left and settled down."

For the first time today, Cale felt a weight shift on his shoulders, not relieved of a heavy burden quite yet, but definitely lighter. Maybe, just maybe, he could find a way to make this work. Dillon intended to. If he could maneuver into a similar position but with local ties, he could be close to Lily. Pursue this budding relationship, watching it and her flower with his attentions.

Quickly chastising himself, he stomped down that possibility. It was an ideal solution in an ideal world. He didn't live in that. Reality came up to bite people in the ass when they least expected it.

"Ready to go court the young lady in the kitchen?" Dillon teased, standing with both crutches for support.

Cale rolled his eyes. "We're outta here. Soon." Anger laced his voice. He quickly stood and turned.

Dillon shook his head. "You wouldn't know what's good for you if it stood there staring you in the face. Besides, have you considered that Lansing's crew might have stumbled across our ditched car? It won't take a genius to track us here. Once we're gone, Lily's vulnerable."

Cale's gut clenched at the thought of what those men would do to the shy and innocent woman who had taken them in. For helping them out in a bind, she would suffer as no one should ever have to. Just the thought of those men touching her stoked a deep-seated rage. Fury rose up, flashing through his veins. He shot Dillon a glare before stepping from the room.

Cale drew in a deep breath, forcing calmness over his raging emotions. *Cool it, SEAL.* Losing control signed a death warrant in his business. In order for him to protect Dillon and Lily, he needed to focus rationally, not go off half-cocked. He'd think of something. He always did. He forced a smile when he entered the kitchen, determined to shield Lily from his caustic mood and sincere worry that killers could show up on their doorstep at any minute.

Chapter Twelve

Charles Lansing slammed his fist down on the table in sheer frustration. His lucrative arms exchange had gone to hell in a hand basket when those military types had shown up and killed two of his best men. Blind luck had saved his life and a couple of others when they'd run late to meet for the exchange.

The Feds? Maybe. It didn't matter. He'd worked too hard for too many years to build his weapons trade business on the black market for anything to get in his way now. Word of mouth carried far. If other customers heard even the barest whisper that he couldn't provide the items promised or that the government was hot on his trail, they would look to his competitors to fill their orders. He couldn't have that. He *wouldn't* have that.

Toby, his best tracker and computer expert, had spent nearly every minute since the ambush trying to ferret out information about the people responsible and their location. They knew one man had been shot. He would require medical attention, so Toby had methodically scoped out hospitals small and large, searching inpatients and emergency rooms in five states, seeking anyone with a bullet wound who would meet the criteria. Nothing as of his last report this morning, but something would turn up. *It had to.* He could be patient a little longer—after all, the risk and reward were both high. It was a game of kill or be killed. Revenge and retaliation.

He wasn't stupid enough to believe that whatever group these two men were with would simply walk away, leaving him to conduct business in peace. Oh, no. They would do everything in their power to see him six feet under. It was the same determination he possessed toward them. Fuckers dared to interfere in his lucrative business.

He'd track them down, corner them, and kill them like rabid animals.

"Sir, we have a location." Toby dashed over. "We found their abandoned vehicle. Tracks and blood drops lead toward Cooperstown."

A slow smile slipped out. *Finally.*

After pulling some maps out, he placed them on the large desk, scouring over them for the destination. Charles grabbed a pencil and began jotting down a list of supplies they would need and potential areas of interest.

Most rural areas had a family doctor. They would start there. Find the doctor, follow the trail. Kill the vermin where they lay in hiding.

Only then could he go back to the business of shipping his highly specialized and powerful weapons to those who had the money to pay for them. He didn't care which side they were on or even which country they resided in. All he wanted was the money, the riches he accrued from those deals. After all, entrepreneurship and making money was the American way.

He grabbed what he needed and placed a quick call to his remaining men. By the time they had rounded up everything, his men were ready and they quickly left the base on a necessary and deadly mission.

* * * *

Several hours later, all three men sauntered into the Cooperstown Diner, seeking two things — hot food and information.

A handful of customers were spread across the small room. Choosing a somewhat isolated table in the back where they could watch the door, Charles sat down. All three glanced over the room, catching the eye of the waitress dressed in an old-fashioned pink dress complete with white apron.

"What can I get you?" she asked, pulling out her pen and ticket pad.

They gave her their orders. Just before she turned toward the kitchen, Charles spoke again, "Miss. My friend here hasn't been feeling too well." He gestured at one of the men across the table. "Is there a local doctor he could see?"

The young blonde girl nodded, then seemed to recall something. "Dr Snider. But he's out this week for the holiday. Went to visit all kinds of family in the next state over or such."

"Oh." Charles pondered a second. "What about his nurse? Maybe she could take care of my friend?"

"Lily? Oh, she's not one of those practitioner nurses. She's just a regular old nurse that helps the doctor. I'm thinking you need to head up the road to Clinton. That's the nearest hospital."

"Thanks. We'll do that after lunch." Charles promised watching the waitress walk off.

Good thing about small towns—everyone knows everyone else's business. From what the girl said, there was no use in chasing a doctor all over creation. But his nurse... Lily.

She could and would provide the information they needed.

Chapter Thirteen

Wednesday morning broke bright and sunny, though a definite chill resided in the air. Not surprising for late November.

Lily pulled herself from the warm pile of blankets and cats all cuddled on the sleeper sofa. Certainly not as comfortable as her bed, but it could have been worse. Not bothering to make her temporary bed with the cats still asleep, she quickly headed to the second bathroom in the hallway right outside the spare bedroom. Since the guys had moved into the master bed and bath, she had contented herself with the smaller guest bathroom. It afforded her a bit more privacy and she didn't have to wake them up when she woke early.

With her hair pulled up in a ponytail, she headed to the kitchen in her warm and comfortable sweats. Baking monopolized her agenda for the day. Pies, cinnamon rolls, and homemade bread. All stood on her list as a must for Thanksgiving lunch.

Carson called just as she was pulling ingredients out for the pie. "How's our patient today?"

"Up and about. Ate like a horse last night. Wound still looks clean. Light pink, just serous drainage with a few spots of blood now and again. The sitz baths have helped, I think. No redness or pus."

"Great. Sounds like you can remove the IV and change him over to the oral antibiotics I sent. Get one more dose in him this morning, then transition him over."

"Okay." She plopped the berries in the sink, cradling her cell phone between her ear and shoulder. "How's the family?"

"Good."

She simpered at his lackluster tone. "Driving you mad, yet?"

Carson snorted. "Almost, but Casey's happy. That's all that counts."

A twinge of envy hit Lily at the absolute love and adoration Carson felt for his wife Casey. Most likely women searched a lifetime for such a complete man, a rock solid relationship, and love that poured from them when they were together. Lily knew she'd read all the fairy tales growing up, had looked around here and there for her version of Prince Charming and come up empty. Spinsterhood seemed more and more likely these days.

"Has Cale been ruffling your feathers?"

The quiet question pulled her from her thoughts. "Not really. He started out pretty intense, but I think we've agreed upon a truce."

"Oh?"

She pulled out a kitchen chair and plopped down, making sure to keep her voice down lest her guests overhear. "Nothing formal, per se. Just an acknowledgment that he pawed through my underwear drawer and a subtle hint at some freaky toe licking fetish."

Warm laughter rang through the phone. She grinned in reaction, pleased with how things had progressed this morning.

"I think you're good for him."

Lily shrugged. "They need rest and care is all."

"True, but that's not what I meant. You're good for Cale. He needs someone to remind him how to laugh, to show him a gentler hand."

"Carson..." She didn't need him to go down that particular path. Heck, she had a hard enough time resisting the journey herself.

"He's a good man, Lily. I'm just saying don't close the door on the idea before you've given it a try."

She sighed. "I don't know. They'll be gone in a few days, anyway."

"Maybe. Maybe not."

A muted voice spoke in the background. "I've got to get going. Call me if you need anything or if Dillon takes a bad turn, though I don't expect he'd do so at this stage in the game."

"Okay."

"Lily, give fate a chance." His words struck a chord deep inside.

"I'll talk to you later." Clicking off the conversation, she slumped back in the chair.

Nosey doctor. She could understand the general questions and inquiries about Dillon and his wound. But he couldn't fool her with his not-so-subtle references to Cale. The man was fishing in an empty pond.

With a shake of her head, she stood up and quickly tossed frozen blueberries into a bowl, adding sugar and flour. After mixing it all up, she began to pour the contents into the ready-made pie shells when Cale walked into the room.

Her belly flip-flopped at the sight of his clean-shaven, handsome face, light blue eyes sparkling, and sleepy expression. Ever since their last kiss, she'd wished for more. Dreamed of what would come next. *If brothers and cats didn't interrupt, that is.*

"Good morning."

"Morning to you, too." She took the wooden spoon and carefully scraped errant berries out of the bowl and into the small mound in the lower pie shell. "I'll get breakfast in a minute. Let me…"

"I'll take care of it."

She paused to look up at his face, catching his indulgent expression. "Are you sure? I don't mind."

He waved her off, opening the fridge to check the contents. "I've fixed more than one meal in my life." A box of mix appeared in his hand along with the milk before he shut the door. "Pancakes I can do."

"Okay. Thanks." She plopped the bowl into the sink then grabbed the top pie shell and carefully placed it over the berries.

"What are the plans for today?" He opened a cabinet and pulled out a medium-sized glass bowl and began to dump in batter, milk, and an egg, whisking them all together with ease of strength and long practice.

Lily watched his hands, marveling at their sureness and ability. What would those same hands feel like on her body, molding to her curves, teasing sensitive areas, and delving into secret places no other man had been? Combine that expertise with soft lips, darting tongue, and a taste of spring rain. Her lower tummy clenched in a pang of longing pleasure.

"Lily?"

The mention of her name broke through her early morning daydream. "Hmmm?"

"Plans? For the day?" Amusement laced his tone while his eyes sparkled as if he read her mind.

Kissing you. Touching you. Checking for that danged belly button. Her face heated. "Oh... Ummm..." Pinching the edges of the pie together, she took a second or two to get her sluggish mind back to spinning. "Plans. Let's see. Get this pie baked. Cinnamon rolls. Maybe a chocolate cake. But I need to start the homemade bread next. That'll take most of the day to get done."

"Skillet?"

Lily reached into the oven, pulling out a small pile of gadgets and necessities, a large skillet included. She quickly handed it over. A tingle sizzled along her nerves when his fingers caressed hers during the exchange.

"Homemade bread? People still do that?" Cale confidently poured batter into the skillet, making small circles after turning on the heat and spraying it.

She nodded. "My mother made bread every year, usually around Christmas, but sometimes more often. You can't imagine the wonderful aroma while it's cooking and how it melts in your mouth, topped with butter."

Setting the bowl aside, Cale met her gaze. A sultry lowering of his eyelids told her he pictured a bit more than eating bread. Her belly flopped once more.

She stepped closer, brushing against his large frame, standing on tiptoe as he lowered his head. No sooner had those gifted lips of his sealed over hers than he pushed his tongue forward, asking for entry. Automatically, she opened farther, not only allowing his inspection, but giving it right back to him.

"What's for breakfast?"

With a muttered curse, Cale stepped back, his expression smoldering.

Lily pulled her attention from him, fighting to still her rapidly beating heart and increased breathing. "Dillon. Cale is...making pancakes." *Making me want to nibble on him, too.*

A knowing grin covered Dillon's face. With practiced ease, he shifted to the table using his crutches and sat down.

"Oh, Carson called. He said that after this morning's IV antibiotic, I can take out that IV and we can give you the tablets he packed in the medical bag. From the way I described the wound, he thought it was healing nicely and you would soon be as good as new." She sent him a small grin, thrilled with his quick recovery.

"Great. It'll be a nice change to not be tied down for nearly an hour at a time, several times a day."

She headed to the cabinet, pulling out plates and glasses while Cale returned to the fridge, and grabbed the butter. Both placed their items on the table.

"I can imagine," she answered, setting the places for breakfast.

Hope's loud cry broke through the kitchen.

"Oh, good grief. Don't tell me she's starving again?" Dillon looked down at the fluffy cat sitting at his feet. She met his eyes before meowing once more. "I guess that answered that."

"Endless pits. All of them. I swear." Lily dug through another cabinet, handing over two cans of cat food to Dillon. "Here you go. You can be their hero this morning."

He snorted, but quickly pivoted on the chair enough to be able to pop the lids and pour the cans of food into three small ceramic dishes. The cats swarmed immediately, wasting no time digging into their breakfast. "They sure like that stuff."

Lily watched them eat heartily. "Yeah. It's expensive, but I can't begin to deny them when they obviously love it."

"You're a good person, Lily," Cale spoke quietly as he placed a plate full of pancakes on the table in front of his brother.

"I just did what any other person would do." She strode over to grab the orange juice out of the fridge, uncomfortable with the rare praise.

Dillon concurred. "He's right. I don't know that I've said it, but thank you for taking us in, feeding us, the nursing care. Everything."

She smiled at him, the bottle of juice on the table. With a deep sigh, she forced the words out of her mouth. "I'm the one that should be thanking you."

Both men looked at her, confusion apparent on their faces. Cale sat down opposite Dillon, studying her carefully.

"I thought this holiday...would be lonely and sad just sitting home alone with no one to talk to, to be with, just my memories to sustain me. Then you guys showed up. It's like a gift or fate or something. I've been having a good time and never once felt lonely. And I thank you for coming to stay with me."

Cale regarded her for a long moment, his gaze flicking over her features, before standing once more. He pulled her flush and gave her a hug.

She felt the brush of lips on her temple and couldn't help but grin at the small show of affection in front of others. A quick glance found Dillon beaming like a kid with a secret. *He'll probably torment Cale later.* The thought only cheered her more. The guys could use all the humor and good-natured ribbing they could handle.

Releasing her, Cale eased back, stealing a quick, chaste kiss. "Eat up. Breakfast is getting cold and you need energy if you're going to do all that baking you spoke of."

"Baking?" Dillon's face lit up.

Lily nodded, taking her seat. "Homemade bread, cinnamon rolls, and pies."

A huge smile covered his face. "Better make extra. Cale doesn't share well."

Cale reached across to smack his brother on the back of the head before sitting down. "Brat."

Both of the guys chuckled while Lily smiled to herself. From being such a surly man she first met, Cale was fast easing into a fun, teasing, and lovable soldier. He took pleasure in Dillon and the love shined through. Maybe, just maybe, she could find a way to keep that smile on his face and flash of mischief in his eyes. Nothing would make her happier.

Chapter Fourteen

Cale trudged along with Lily, walking through the pasture, crunching through long grass nearly done for the season, checking fences and cattle as they went. He lagged just behind her, giving him a nice view of a shapely rear while allowing him to cover her if any danger popped up. He kept a vigil while she fussed over that bull, just in case the beast got his dander up. Like before, he behaved like a big lap dog, eager for any treat or affection she lavished on him. Not that he blamed the old bull. He would rub against her too, begging her to run those hands over his body, not stopping until all his itches had been satisfied.

She had set the homemade bread up earlier, declared that it needed time to rise, tossed on that old threadbare coat, and headed out for her chores.

Although Lily had protested mildly at his unwavering intention to accompany her, Cale insisted on tagging along for a couple of reasons. He enjoyed their time together, her quirky sense of humor, and simply sharing the beautiful autumn days with someone who could appreciate the small gifts in life.

She banished the darkness for a while with her bright nature, pushing aside all memories of his cruel past and brutal experiences both before and after war. He found the positive energy addictive and couldn't resist sampling the salvation she offered.

The other reason was that his gut told him Lansing and his gang had to be closing in while he and Dillon holed up with Lily. Once they got a bead on Cooperstown, it wouldn't take them long to connect the dots to her. Before then, Dillon and Cale had to be gone and a foolproof plan had to be in place to keep Lily safe from those bastards. So far, he kept running into dead ends. The best scenario he found was to stay with her and fight it out. Yet, he dared not expose her to that danger. Once the realization hit of what he actually did and how he did it, Lily would turn from him in disgust and fear. She was too tender-hearted, too soft for that kind of life, even for a brief flicker in time. He couldn't repay her generosity with a gun battle, putting her in the line of fire, damaging her home — giving her forever memories of the horrors of battle that would seep into dreams more often than not. He could vouch for that disturbing fact himself.

What am I going to do?

"Look." Lily stopped and pointed to his right.

A small red fox stood at the edge of wooded brush, partially concealed. He seemed content enough to watch them, but Cale knew if they headed in his direction, he would duck through the debris, disappearing in a split second. "There are a lot of foxes here?" He glanced to the wild canine once more before focusing his attention ahead.

She shook her head. "Not many. I only see one now and again." Stepping forward, she made the turn for home.

He watched her movements, graceful and sure. Despite her continued insistence that she was only average and clumsy, he simply couldn't see it. Her body may not have compared with a runway model, but those were way too thin, anyway. He enjoyed women with a bit more meat on their flesh. She didn't have to be an athlete, but one that could keep up with his energy levels. Lily fit that bill. More than that, her inner strength and kindness added another strong draw. He couldn't remember the last woman he had been with that had half the compassion as this one. Her giving nature scarcely existed in today's world, making her a precious and rare gemstone, one that he wanted to polish, shine, and cherish.

I'm turning into a damn marshmallow, he scolded himself, pulling away from such thoughts. "You moved here in February, right?"

"Yep."

"Why hadn't you gotten a pet before Hope showed up? It's obvious how much you love animals." He noticed each evening she held the big cat, talked tenderly to her, and snuggled away. More than once, she tucked Hope under the covers, keeping the cat toasty on the cool nights. The kittens normally wouldn't sit still long enough to enjoy such pampering, but they never lacked for attention or affection from their owner. No one could love their child more than Lily loved those cats.

She paused to let him move abreast. "When I first moved here, there was so much to do, getting the house and my life in order. Work kept me busy. Spring arrived before I had a chance to breathe. I begged Carson to allow me to plant a garden, just like my mother and I used to do. He agreed, even got Cody to come over and till for me. That kept me hopping with planting and weeding. Then the vegetables needed picking and canning..."

"That would explain the garden and all those jars of canned vegetables in the pantry."

Lily nodded. "It was something my mother and I did each year. Worked in the garden together and canned. It was...peaceful."

He saw the emotions appear on her face. A twinge of pain painted her features before she took a deep breath and lifted her chin. "Anyway, I always had intentions of getting a pet. At first a dog, but I didn't think I was home enough to be fair to him or her. They can only be expected to cross their legs for so long. Then, I considered a cat, but somehow the time never seemed right, or when it did, I didn't have the extra money to pay the adoption fee."

"So fate intervened?" He reached down, brushing her fingers with his. She responded by linking their hands.

"You could say that." A smile brightened her expression where sadness had resided moments before. "She's a pricey girl, but more than worth it. I'll have to get her and the girls spayed next month, before Hope comes into heat again. If I don't have enough saved up for the kittens, they can wait a bit longer until I have the funds." She rambled on as if she were simply thinking out loud.

He shortened his steps to compensate for her shorter legs. "Aren't Faith and Charity too young for spaying? I thought they had to be six months or something like that."

"Oh, that was the old adage. But, from what I understand, vets do the surgery on much younger animals, particularly kittens and puppies up for adoption, ensuring it gets done and no further homeless babies will be born to those animals."

Cale nodded, scanning the area once more.

"What will you do after your present job? Have any dreams to follow?" Lily picked at a tall clump of grass as she passed.

Dreams? A man like me? Holding in a snort at such an idea, he flipped through a few possible answers. In all honesty, he didn't expect to live long enough to worry about dreams and retirement. Not many in his profession did. It was equivalent to asking a kindergartener what they wanted to be when they grew up. Some may have been able to give an answer, but very few thought seriously about it beforehand. Getting a job and following a career were so far off to those kids, they had no real idea what they wanted to do. Same way with guys like him. They didn't delve too deeply into something that existed only with a bit of luck and would be so far in the future, it seemed trivial in the present. Wishes didn't get one anywhere. Hard work and sacrifice did.

Lily lived an innocent life. She still believed that dreams and miracles existed. He would do everything in his power to keep it that way, shielding her from his own violent nature and men like Lansing who would cut to the chase, doling out as much cruelty as necessary to get information in the fastest means possible.

"That must be quite the list of dreams you have."

Her soft amused voice drew him back to her original question. "I really don't have any dreams. Live in the present. That's how we...I live. As far as leaving my job, I haven't thought that far ahead." *Cop out.* Drowning in her hazel eyes, he answered more truthfully. "Okay. I have considered the option, but haven't come up with another occupation that I might fit and not be bored to insanity or fired for attitude."

"Hmmm." Lily tapped her chin. "Ever considered porn star?"

He never would have expected that suggestion from her. Her lips twitched until she lost the battle and burst out laughing. He followed suit, chuckling and marveling at her ability to turn his morose moods into merriment. Arching an eyebrow at her, he squeezed her hand. "You've been picturing me as a porn star?"

A flush appeared across her face as she lowered her head.

His grin widened. Teasing her proved to be a fun, addictive hobby. Those delightful blushes rewarded him each time, making him wonder just how low that crimson tint went over her body. He surged forward. "So, what am I wearing in those porn star dreams?"

Her color deepened. Like a fish, her mouth opened and closed several times without a sound emerging.

He tugged a strand of long blonde hair with his free hand. "I'm just teasing. You're so easy. Besides, those blushes are quite pretty."

She gave him a shove. "Neanderthal."

That didn't put a dent into his playfulness.

Instead, it sealed the deal. Words he never expected to hear again rang inside his head.

I want her. By my side. For good.

* * * *

As soon as they returned to the house, Lily excused herself to start preparing more cinnamon rolls. Cale went to check on Dillon.

His brother sat on the edge of the bed, head in his hands. His ever-present pistol rested on top of the comforter.

Concerned, Cale hurried over, kneeling to be eye level, tugging at Dillon's wrists. "What is it? Are you in pain?"

Dillon met his gaze. His usual twinkling eyes filled with frustration and worry. "Mayberry called while you were outside with Lily," Dillon whispered making sure Lily couldn't overhear their conversation.

"And?"

"Seems a trio of tough-looking men pulled into Cooperstown late last night, stopped by the local diner and started asking to see the local doctor. One of the waitresses told him the office was closed, but they ferreted out names, including Lily's."

Cale sucked in his breath, understanding all that wasn't said.

"Mayberry didn't know anything else, but he was worried. Told me where his stash of weapons is kept in case we need them."

"Shit." Cale ran one hand through his hair, fear and fury warring inside. They would have already learned Carson was out of town and focus their attention on Lily. Hell, they could be on the way to the house as they spoke. One hand scrubbed over his face as he scrambled for ideas.

"Dillon, did you remember to take..." Lily's voice dropped off when she noticed them. "What's wrong?"

"Tell her," Dillon commanded. "She has a right to know."

"No. This doesn't..."

Dillon cut through his reply. "Tell her, damn, it."

Cale growled at his brother before turning his attention back to Lily. Regret and rage raced to the fore. "We didn't kill all of our targets. The survivors are probably hot on our trail and will destroy anyone that stands in their way for revenge."

"Why didn't you tell me this before? I'm not some weak chit that would fall into hysterics at the drop of a hat." Her body tensed, hands cutting through the air in jerky motions as she spoke.

"I didn't want you to experience the horrors of our reality. You're so full of cheer and joy, I couldn't take that away from you, replacing it with fear and loathing." *Damn, it. It's true.*

"You believed that I would turn my back on you, thinking you are some licensed killer?" At his silence, she shook her head. "Soap for brains, I swear." Hands on hips, she took a deep breath. "I'm not naïve enough to believe bad things don't happen. People don't show up in a doctor's office carrying a bullet on accident. I had a good idea from day one what you did, but didn't think less of you. Instead, I commended you for having the guts to do such a job, taking out the leeches of the human world to keep the rest of us safe. I still do. You're brave and have more courage than King Solomon had wives. However, you must think I'm some frail idiot who would faint at the sight of a snake in order to decide never to tell me what was going on. Sure, I believe you guys can protect me, but I deserve to know that not only am I in danger, but my girls are, too. You don't keep that kind of information from me. I'll do whatever it takes, including shooting to kill, in order to protect what is mine. Come hell or high water." Finished with her rant, she pivoted on her heel and stormed out of the room, still muttering under her breath.

Watching her go, Cale checked his own anger, reminding himself he did it for her own good, to protect her from the cruel world he lived in each and every day.

Dillon whistled low. "Whoa. Talk about fiery."

Cale shrugged, still focused on the trail Lily had taken out of the room.

"Makes a man hard as a rock wondering where else that fire might burn."

Smacking his brother on the back of the head, Cale snarled, "She's off limits."

"Uh-huh. For you, too?"

Not bothering to answer, Cale marched away, seething and well chastised. She had a valid point. He could see that through the haze of anger. But, damn it to hell. She didn't deserve this, being put in such a position for simply having the decency to take in an injured man and nurse him back to health. It wasn't fair. *Since when is life fair?* Lily had a right to her anger, but it didn't change things. He would've done the same thing again. But now that she knew, the least he could do was be more open with her.

He found her in the laundry room, tossing clothes into the washer.

"I was involved the moment you walked through Carson's door. I knew it just like I know the sun will rise every morning in the east."

"I know. And, for the record, I'm sorry. I wanted to spare you this. I thought—"

"That if you and Dillon left quickly, those bad guys would lose your trail?" Her calm and rational words clashed with her fury of moments before.

He nodded. "I hoped to be on the road, the sooner the better, leaving you to your life without the worry of being caught in the crossfire."

She released a sigh. "They would have found me, anyway. It doesn't take a genius, once they whittle it down to Cooperstown, to find Carson and me."

Cale moved closer, pulling her into his arms, tucking her head against his chest. His stomach sank at the thoughts of what Lansing and his gang would do to her, if they got their hands on her. "I know. I know we can't leave now. But, I swear by all that is holy, I will protect you." *I will die before I let them put one finger on her.*

She squirmed, earning a bit of breathing room from his tight clutches. "I can take care of myself, soldier boy. Give me my Glock. I can hit center target every time."

He frowned down at her. "This isn't target shooting. Killing a man is difficult and there's always consequences, even for seasoned soldiers."

With a small nod, she leaned back against his frame. "I can do what I have to. Always have, always will. Promise."

He dipped his head and pressed a kiss to her crown, reveling in the moment of holding her tight, and praying nothing happened to this small miracle on earth. He would never forgive himself if she paid the price for his stupidity. "I'll keep you safe. Those cats of yours, too."

His chest tingled at the small motion of her lips turning up into a smile against his pectoral muscles. If only he could hold her skin to skin, no clothes to interfere with even the slightest sensation. Take care of the present, then, just maybe, he could dream of the future. *A future with Lily.*

"Bad guys or not, we're having Thanksgiving."

Cale's mouth twitched with her declaration. "So there," he finished for her. Unable to resist, he tilted up her chin, sought her lips, and covered them with his own. "And, for the record, it's Navy SEAL, not soldier."

Chapter Fifteen

The alarm clock beeped loudly beside Lily's ear where she stashed it in the night for fear of waking up the guys. Thanksgiving morning. Four a.m. With a groan, she forced herself to move, knowing she had to get the turkey in the oven now or it wouldn't be done in time for lunch. The last thing she wanted to do was serve an undercooked bird for their feast after all this work. Besides, this might be the last meal Cale and Dillon shared with her, leaving afterwards to who knows where, fighting the ancient battle of good versus evil. That sobering thought pushed her into action.

A full moon shined brightly through the kitchen window, illuminating enough of the room that she only had to turn on a small light located under the cabinet. No sense in wasting electricity and waking the dead with all the lights on at such an early time.

Luckily, she had prepared everything the night before, so all she had to do was stick the bird in the oven. *Dang heavy thing.* With a final push, she managed to center it on the rack. She shut the door, and pushed the button to the correct temperature. She stepped to the sink, washing her hands under the warm water while gazing out of the window.

Movement within the shadows behind the huge oak tree caught her attention. Not much, but just enough for her to realize it wasn't anything natural. Sounds of restless cattle came to the fore as they paced and shifted, preparing to bolt if the need arose.

She rushed to the bedroom, heading straight for her bedside table.

"What is it?" Cale spun around from his position at the bedroom window.

Dillon sat up immediately, pulling himself to the side of the bed.

"Probably nothing. Something is upsetting the cattle. Last time they did this, it was a pack of wild dogs." She sincerely hoped that was the case. If it was those men Cale had spoken of... A shiver ran down her back at the mere thought.

She wrapped her hand around the Glock. Before she could spin around once more, Cale reached out to stop her.

"Stay here." Kneeling down, he fished for, then yanked out one of their large duffles, pulling out a couple of handguns and a rifle, handing the latter to Dillon. "We'll go check it out."

Lily stared at him in stunned silence. Guns didn't bother her. She'd been raised with them and taught to shoot at an early age, compliments of a beat cop for a father. Even seeing the amount and complexity of their weapons didn't faze her. It was the expression that came over both men—serious, deadly, intimidating. Any man looking at them from the other side of a gun would swear he stared at the devil himself.

With a headshake, she pulled herself back to the present situation. "No. This is my house and I'm responsible for those cattle. Besides, if it's wild dogs, I prefer you don't kill them. They are simply hungry and looking for an easy meal. You can't blame them for that. I just run them off. No biggie. If it's not, I'll be right there with you."

Both men ignored her, going about their preparations with efficiency.

"If you can see them from the kitchen, they're coming in from the south. I'll go out the front and snake around the east, see if I can locate them." Cale tightened his grip on his weapon.

Dillon nodded. "I'll cover you from the back. If you have to backtrack, give me a sec to change positions. I'm taking those bastards out once and for all."

"I'm going with you."

"No. You stay here. You'll only be in the way."

Frustrated, Lily glared at both of them. "I know what I'm doing."

Cale leveled his gaze, biting off each word. "Those aren't four-legged predators out there. Like I told you yesterday, we didn't clean out that vipers' nest completely. Some escaped. They'll be hot on our heels and determined to send us to hell and anyone else along the way. This is what we do. Let us do what we're trained to do."

"He's right. Let's roll."

"But your leg..." Lily protested only to have Dillon silence her with a glare.

"May slow me down a hair, but that's all." He tugged Lily's pajama sleeve, indicating that she should follow him, sticking to the dark. Her Glock remained at the ready, although at this point she hadn't a clue what good it would do. Between the three handguns she knew Cale carried and Dillon's rifle, it would take an army to make it inside for her to even have a chance to nick one.

Cale disappeared out of the front, the door shutting silently behind him.

She sent up a quick prayer that he would return safe and sound, fear twisting her belly into a ball, realizing that he could be killed right before her eyes. If such a horrific event happened, she would never have another opportunity to express her feelings for him.

Dillon led her back to the kitchen, motioned for her to remain silent and out of sight.

Tense moments passed while Lily sat and waited for something, anything to happen. The waiting and suspense put her on the brink of anxiety. She forced the panic down, hoping to absorb the confidence Dillon showed.

This can't be happening. People like her didn't find themselves in the middle of some gun battle with criminals. They lived boring and dull lives. Each year, they cooked Thanksgiving dinner and the largest worry they had would be if the turkey was dry or undercooked. If they should put the stuffing inside the bird or cook it separate to help prevent food poisoning. If she wanted the gun and knife club, she would have moved to the big city and worked at a large hospital, seeing victim after victim enter through those emergency room doors covered in blood and fighting to survive. No. Her life was supposed to be calm and peaceful, living with her cats in the middle of nowhere, growing a vegetable garden and watching baby bunnies eat her cherry tomatoes. All too surreal, she blinked at her current situation, grasping at her wits.

Dillon kept vigil out of the window, every once in a while moving smoothly to check out other vantage points. With stealth and graceful motions, he watched outside, more than once raising his rifle to look down the scope.

She started to get up only to find Dillon's hand on her shoulder shoving her back down. His narrowed eyes spared her a split second as he once more raised the rifle into position, obviously prepared to fire directly through her window if the need arose.

Long minutes passed in total silence. No gunshots rang, no sounds of a struggle. Just damning silence that ate at her gut and kept her on edge, barely able to sit still and wait for an outcome, either good or bad.

Just when her stretched nerves threatened to break, a sharp whistle broke the air, resembling the cry of a hawk soaring in the sky. Another followed, this time, the cry of a purple martin. Finally, a quail answered.

Perplexed, Lily slid closer to the front door, eager to peek out and discover what the obvious signals meant.

"Stand down," Dillon called, lowering his rifle, though still grasping it close. His gaze left the window to glance her direction. "That's the all clear. You can set your weapon down now."

With a nod, Lily lightly placed the Glock on the kitchen countertop, anxiously waiting to see what happened next. Dozens of questions raced through her mind, demanding answers.

A click of the front door signaled Cale's return. Racing over, Lily threw herself into his arms, hugging him with the strength of her feelings for him and the immense relief that he appeared safe and sound. Leaning back, she quickly surveyed him for damage. Seeing none, she hugged him all the tighter.

Cale wrapped an arm around her, squeezing in return. He used his free hand to slip the dull black handgun back into the holster at his lower back. "I'm okay." Air brushed against her ear as he whispered to her.

"I was so worried." She felt a kiss to the top of her head and basked happily.

Dillon hobbled over, gimpy but without the assistance of his crutches, flicking the kitchen light on. "Warriors?"

Cale nodded, releasing Lily, a wry grin on his face. "Surprised the hell out of me, too. Nearly stumbled over Night lying in wait. Good thing he's on our side or I would have had a fight on my hands."

Dillon chuckled, looking to the front door. "Where is he?"

"Gathering in the others."

"Others?" Lily's head spun from the turn of events and names she couldn't begin to recognize.

"Our team. Spoon, Night, and Loco."

"But how —?" A knock at the front door interrupted her.

Cale walked over, opening the door wide, gesturing in three men. Lily stared in amazement. All three stood around the same height, big, strong, and full of muscles. Two had short hair in varying shades of brown, and matching eyes. The third sported blue-black hair, hanging past his shoulders, and contained in a ponytail holder. Deep blue eyes made for a striking contrast. Native American heritage shouted loudly from his coloring and facial features.

Just like when Carson and Cale stood over Dillon, Lily felt dwarfed, like a wallaby amongst kangaroos. "Oh, boy. Let me guess. None of you had any difficulty climbing that wall in basic training," Lily muttered as she tilted her head back to look up at them.

The lot chuckled. "No, ma'am."

Cale pulled her against his side. "This is our team. Loco. Spoon. And the boss, Night. This is Lily, Dillon's nurse, babysitter, maid."

Each man gave a brief nod in turn, their predatory appearance diminished only slightly by the happy expressions on their faces.

She elbowed Cale in the side while Dillon snorted.

"Damn, Bugle. Heard you were hit," the one introduced as Loco asked.

Dillon nodded. "Yeah, but I'm on the mend. Been holing up for a few days with nothing to do but take meds and eat."

"Good to know."

"Lansing?" Dillon asked, his question directed at the three newcomers.

Spoon explained. "Yeah. Seems he and his goons arrived Tuesday, looking for first the doctor, then for Lily. They managed to track you guys down that far."

Cale tensed next to her, pulling her flush with his body.

Night took up the tale. "Daughter of the doctor's receptionist owns the diner."

"Lisa?" Lily asked.

He nodded.

"Lisa is in the National Guard. She's sharp and capable," Lily quickly informed them, boasting about the assets of her friend.

The sandy-haired man stepped forward. "Seems she got a bad feeling when these guys started asking about you and the doc. So she called her mother, who called the doc. Good old Mayberry pulled some strings, but finally found the person to make contact with Night. He thought you guys could take care of yourselves and anyone else, but decided back-up couldn't hurt."

"How close?" Dillon eased to one of the kitchen chairs, lines of pain crossing his face.

"Caught up with them on the side road, about a mile away. Armed to the gills, but what else would you expect of that son of a bitch? Tango Uniform now."

She didn't understand any of their terminology, but figured everything was on the up and up or they wouldn't be standing in her living room making introductions. "I didn't hear anything." *If they were that close, I would have heard gunshots, right?*

"You wouldn't have." Cale gave her a squeeze.

"Clean-up?"

"Done." Spoon answered in a low tone.

"I owe you." Sincerity filled Cale's words.

The guys shrugged it off. "You would have done the same for us." Loco slapped Cale on the back.

Silence filled the room. Night tilted his head toward the door. "We should be off." The other men lined up, preparing to leave.

"Wait!" Lily reached out to stop them.

They turned in unison.

"Please. Don't go. I'm fixing Thanksgiving lunch and assuming it's edible... There should be plenty. I would like for you to stay and eat with us. Please? It's the least I can do for what you've done."

Night glanced toward Cale who shrugged. The others waited in silence.

"Did I mention I have homemade bread and cinnamon rolls?" She crossed her fingers, hoping the lure of the baked goods would tilt the scale in her favor.

Each man shared a look before smiling. "I think we can do that."

* * * *

A few hours later, her kitchen bustled with activity. Even the newest guests refused to allow her to do most of the work, claiming they couldn't sit on their rears and allow her to run herself to a lather trying to cook for a small herd of men. Spoon took a position at the stove, working on the vegetables, while Night mashed potatoes. Loco and Cale retrieved the table leaves from under her bed, set them in place, and brought in the two spare chairs from the second bedroom. Dillon rounded up the kittens, keeping them entertained and out from under people's feet lest they got stepped on.

Spinning, she barely missed Loco as he pulled dishes and silverware out for the meal. Her tiny kitchen overflowed with people, but that didn't deter the guys from doing their part.

She analyzed and directed, amazed at the abilities of the guys. Rumor had it most men wouldn't step foot in a kitchen to cook unless they held careers as chefs or simply loved to prepare meals. Yet, here stood five tall, dark, handsome, and deadly men, cutting, slicing, cleaning, and mashing as if they cooked often.

Home. She wondered if they even had one. Like everyone else, they probably had a place they called theirs, to drop off their clothes, pick up bills, and sleep occasionally. A house, sure, but a house didn't always make a home.

Through cordial chit-chat, she discovered that none of them were married and they had all been in the military at some point in their lives. No surprise considering what little she knew about the job they did now. *Too bad for the women of the world.* Despite their dangerous nature and intimidating appearance, they really behaved like true gentlemen. They toiled right along with her, no laziness in any of their bones as they all worked together toward placing a nice feast on the table.

A woman could do worse, much worse. Sure, nothing was ever perfect, but having a hunky man with gentle hands, a kind nature, the ability to cook, clean, and protect was the stuff of dreams.

Her gaze fell on Cale. *Definitely the stuff of dreams.* If only she could be sure he felt the same.

The chime of a timer brought her back to reality. The turkey was done.

With all the help from the guys, a feast soon lay before them. Cale carved the turkey, while the group commented on his knife-handling skills, tossing out comments and comparisons, not all of them positive or flattering. Lily couldn't be sure, but she thought he might have given them a one-fingered wave between slices.

"Scavengers," Night announced from his seat at the end of the table.

Lily looked down. Sure enough, Hope and her kittens had smelled the hot food and marched right over, sitting between the men, outright begging for table scraps. Dillon swore he had worn them out playing, but leave it to her bunch to find energy when food appeared. Beaming, she hopped up to grab a couple of paper towels. Cale anticipated her move, cut two thin slices of turkey and laid them gently on the towels. Calling the girls, she lured them away from the table and over to their feeding station. She quickly pulled the tender meat apart with her fingers, cautioning the cats their food was still hot.

"It's easier to give up and feed them first than to try to keep them off the table. Besides, they have that downright pitiful starvation look down pat." Dillon tossed out the information as he passed a bowl full of mashed potatoes around.

Watching the girls eat with their usual haste, Lily moved back to Cale's spot in the kitchen. "I think we're going to need a couple more pieces to fill them up."

She tore the turkey into smaller chunks, spreading the meal out before the fur babies. "They should sleep well this afternoon with such full tummies."

"Just like people?" Spoon shoveled in a mouthful of homemade bread. She had warmed a whole loaf, figuring the guys might plow right through it.

"Here, I thought men didn't sleep. They watch football, unbutton their pants, pass gas, belch, and scratch their...parts after such a meal," Lily teased, the heat rising in her face when she realized what she'd almost said.

Loco grinned at her. "Pert near."

Lily couldn't wipe the smile off her face. Never would she have imagined her first Thanksgiving alone would be just the opposite of what she had envisioned a week ago. Cats with bulging bellies lay around bathing and napping. Five oversized men sat at the table, shoveling in food while reminiscing and teasing, more like a family than simple co-workers. Each and every one of them thanked her, sincerely appreciating the effort and meal. Though dangerous and probably deadly, these men made her feel safe, honored, and humbled. Golden hearts resided under their thick layers of skin.

The chatter died down as everyone worked on cleaning their plates. Large mounds of vegetables disappeared by the spoonful as the platter of turkey slowly whittled down to scraps. Just as Lily had expected, the homemade bread soon bit the dust. Even the desserts vanished nearly as fast as she could pass out utensils and bowls.

Declaring themselves stuffed, all the guys chipped in to clean up the kitchen. Dillon even washed dishes, mainly because Cale left him no choice, threatening to kick his rear if he didn't get to the task and quit whimpering about it. She couldn't help but roll her eyes at the interplay with the brothers. More than once one of them would smack the other for some presumed insult. Just like when they were kids, she would bet. Their poor mother must have considered them a great handful.

Within thirty minutes, her kitchen sparkled. Clean dishes were put away and trash carried out. Even the floor shined after Loco zipped over it with a hardwood floor mop. The room had never looked better. Thanks to all the guys, who now drifted toward the couch, turning on the small television to watch football. *How typically male.*

She wondered if they would nap and snore, or get all excited about the game and actually pass gas and scratch themselves. Shaking her head, she followed them into the living room, more than happy with the additional surprise guests and the roaring success of the meal. Never once did loneliness or sadness invade her mind. With all the bantering and teasing, she had more than enough distractions and entertainment for sadness to take hold.

Surveying the room, she cringed. For the first time, her spartan furniture and lack of essentials embarrassed her. Night and Loco put her sleeper sofa back together, making room for three of them. Dillon took the small recliner, easing it back to elevate his wounded leg. That left Spoon without a seat except on the hard wooden floor. "I'll get one of the kitchen chairs, although they won't be comfortable..."

He shook his head at her. "I'm fine. Really."

A flick of the wrist sent a couple of pillows from Cale to his comrade. Spoon grinned at him, then made a small nest, placing the cushion on the floor.

That left her. She knew without a doubt any one of the guys would gladly get up, giving up his seat to her. But she didn't want that. They needed some downtime. If watching football after eating Thanksgiving lunch provided that, then she would relish it and let them absorb as much relaxation as they could get.

Cale patted his lap. "Come on."

She looked at him in surprise.

A wicked grin appeared. "I promise to keep my hands to myself and not bite."

"You better. First time you fondle my ass, you'll wonder what bus ran you over," Loco flung at Cale.

Cale flashed his middle finger. "Asshole."

"I'll remember that, football bat."

"Where's a referee when you need one?" Lily snapped her head around, her attention bouncing from one man to another as they mouthed back and forth.

Both shot her a look, pointing to Night, who simply rolled his eyes, shaking his head at their antics. The quiet one, he spoke rarely, but what he did say made her smile. A man of few words, lots of action, and a gentle old soul to those he deemed worthy. She read those truths in his oddly colored eyes.

Shaking her head, Lily stepped around long legs and big feet until she reached Cale. Gingerly, she sat down on his thighs, leaning half against him and half against the armrest, trying to give Loco more room.

Cale immediately wrapped an arm about her, pulling her snug against his side. "There. See. We fit just fine and Loco won't get the tar knocked out of him."

"As if." A loud snort followed.

Dillon clicked on the remote, found the right channel, and everyone turned their attention to the television, focusing on the game.

Lily settled into Cale, soaking up his warmth and strength. A year ago if someone had told her she would be cuddling on a man's lap watching sports with him and his buddies on this holiday, she would have called that person demented. Yet, here she sat, content and even happy. Her heart swelled with emotion, particularly when it came to the man holding her.

He met her eyes and gave her a slight squeeze and a smile, before returning his attention to the game.

For the first time in many months, she felt cared for.

Not to be left out, the girls meandered over. Charity hopped onto Dillon's legs, while Faith marched purposely to Spoon's side, flopping down as if she belonged there. Both men grinned, immediately stroking the kittens. Hope took a bit longer, finally jumping on Night's legs, staring up at him for the longest moment. He spoke to her in a language Lily had never heard before. The cat must have understood as she turned three circles, then settled into a neat ball to doze while the boss of the group lightly brushed her back with long fingers. Three motors began to purr in contentment.

Resting her head on Cale's shoulder, she closed her eyes. *Perhaps there is such a thing as love at first sight after all. At least by second sight, anyway.*

Chapter Sixteen

A shifting movement pulled Lily from her doze. A man's strong arms cradled her body as they gently placed her on bare couch cushions. She woke up with voices nearby, ones it took an extra second to recognize.

In a flash, she sat up, noticing the guys heading toward the front door. "Wait. Are you leaving already?" Her voice croaked, hoarse from her nap. They couldn't go, not now. Not when her relationship with Cale had begun to blossom.

Cale turned to her. "The guys need to get going. Dillon is packing right now."

Her heart sank at his words. She chastised herself for falling for a man that would walk out of her life in mere minutes. *I was just a fill-in for a few short days.*

Cale tugged her against his chest. "I'm not leaving, Lily."

Blinking back tears, she managed to look up into his face, finding the truth she needed. "But you said they were leaving and Dillon was packing."

He nodded, brushing a kiss to her temple. "They're going to drop Dillon by Della's house. He moped and whimpered and looked downright pitiful enough that the guys decided to put him out of his misery."

"Huh?"

A soft grin appeared on Cale's face. "Della only lives about an hour from here. Just past Timberline. Since he was up and about and the danger has passed, Dillon insisted he would get to her tonight, one way or another."

Letting out a relieved breath, Lily returned his smile. "Good for him." She wiggled loose, heading toward the small group of men gathered near the south side of the house, all carrying duffle bags and weapons. "Are you sure you can't stay?"

Spoon shook his head. "Bugle here is determined to get to his woman. Besides, we would only cramp Cale's style hanging around." A twinkle sparked in his eye as he glanced at the man in question.

Cale flipped him off, but quickly ruined the effect with a chuckle.

Dillon limped out of the bedroom carrying his gear. Plopping it down, he headed over to Lily, giving her a warm hug. "Thank you. For everything."

"You're welcome. You remembered the rest of your medication, right?" The nurse in her rose to the occasion.

"Yep. Cale personally checked my bag three times just to make sure." A huge grin spread across his face. "We're headed to Della's."

"I heard." She leaned in to kiss his cheek. "Take care of that girl of yours."

"Will do."

She took a moment to hug each man, thanking them one more time for what they did in protecting Cale, Dillon, and her.

Cale slapped his teammates on the back and wrapped Dillon in a brotherly hug, then stood behind her as together they watched the SUV drive up, the guys pile in, and finally drive off.

A forlorn sigh escaped from Lily.

"What was that sigh about?" Cale spun her around in his arms, shut the door with a free hand, and tilted her chin.

"I miss them already," she confessed.

His lips twitched. "I'm still here."

"I see that." She peered up at him through her lashes, coyly teasing. "So, what are we going to do now?"

"Oh, I can think of a few things," he tossed out, rubbing his chin over her crown. "Walking fences and checking cattle."

"Done that already."

"So we have. Feeding and playing with bottomless pit kittens."

Both turned their attention to the couch, where the small family had taken up residence on the still warm cushions. "I think they're good."

"Laundry and cleaning up the kitchen." His lips teased her earlobe, nibbling with the slightest nip of teeth.

A shiver sped down her spine. "Already done, too." Her voice dropped to a whispery level, sultry with a hint of uncertainty. "Perhaps we can work more on those kisses while I check to make sure you do have a belly button."

His soft laughter sent her hopes flying. Cale reached down, captured her hand, and placed it at the bottom of his T-shirt. "Check anything you want. Anywhere you want."

She sucked on her bottom lip for a long second, new at this game. "What about the kisses?"

He placed a small peck on the end of her nose. "Oh, there will be lots of those. Every kind of kiss imaginable."

Her belly did a slow summersault as his lips sealed over hers. Cale licked the seams of her lips then pressed for entry.

Cale caught her low moan as she melted into his kiss. He wrapped his arms around her, pulling her flush to his frame, allowing her to feel what exactly she did to him. Her hands tugged at his shirt, pulling upward in a near frantic motion.

Breaking their contact, he eased back to remove the article himself, reveling in the expression on her face as she took in his bare chest. No one had ever made him feel handsome and special, not the way Lily did with her rapt attention, appreciation, and obvious enjoyment in staring at him. His blood ran hotter with the realization that such a basic thing appealed so much to her. His cock began to throb, sensing the time had finally arrived. He'd struggled with his heightened libido since he admitted to checking Lily's underwear drawer and heard her accuse him of a fucking foot fetish. Just like she'd slipped under his guard, his body responded in kind, hot and hard, impatient for him to make Lily his.

Almost cautiously, Lily reached out, tenderly placing both hands on his shoulders, allowing them to slowly meander across his pecs, down his sternum, and over his abdomen, excitement and open curiosity sparkled in her eyes the whole time. She sucked on her bottom lip as one finger traced the waistband of his sweats.

The sheer innocence she exuded was the only thing that kept his control in check. As it was, he hauled back on the reins of his control more than once, each little action on her part pushing him further into the flames, while testing his patience. Yet, he'd no more rush this joining than he would walk away leaving them both frustrated and in blazing need. No, she trusted him, he saw the truth in her expression, and he could do nothing less than make their first time a glorious experience to remember for years to come.

Swooping in, he took her mouth once more, his kiss deep and thorough, entreating her to follow him into the fire so they could burn together. He latched onto her sweatshirt, sneaking underneath to lightly stroke and explore until he found her bra-clad breasts. Upon cupping each in a hand, he lightly stroked his thumbs across the nipples, feeling the shiver course through her body as if it was his own. After snaking one hand to her back, he unclasped her bra, eagerly pushing it down and away, far enough to feel her bare skin against his callous roughened palms.

She arched into his touch, a small whimper escaping her mouth only to be caught by his.

Mirroring her with a growl of his own, he stepped back, putting enough space between them so that he could easily read her face. "Are you sure?" He had to make sure because if his suspicions were correct, Lily was about to surrender her virginity. To him.

She nodded, leaning back toward him.

Relief washed through him. The words would have been better, but he read the truth in her face. She wanted him. Wanted this. His arousal jumped tenfold.

He reached out, took one of her small hands, and led her into the bedroom, quietly shutting the door all but a crack behind them. Turning, he took in the sight of Lily as she pulled her bra through one of the sleeves of her sweatshirt. She still wore too many clothes, but he chided himself to go slowly, introduce her with patience and attention to details.

Her gaze roamed over his body once more, pausing an extra beat at the level of his groin. A telling blush appeared.

"Like what you see?" He couldn't resist the urge to tease her.

Lily sucked her bottom lip in a nervous gesture he'd recently discovered. The motion endeared her all the more. "Can I...?" The crimson stain on her face deepened.

"Yes," he answered, not certain what she was asking. It didn't matter. She could do anything she wanted. *Everything she wanted.* He was a willing subject for all her experiments. He stood still, watching her approach slowly, as she reached out for the tie on his sweatpants. No sooner than her fingers touched the string did she peek up, uncertainty written all over her face.

Unable to speak, Cale wrapped his hand over hers, then leisurely tugged, releasing the bow. Still holding her hand, he led it back to his body, tucking her fingers beneath the now loosened waistband.

She wiggled her fingers, lightly stroking his already hard flesh.

The light caress over his sensitive tip nearly sent Cale right over the edge. Cale clamped his back teeth together, holding tightly to his control, giving her the time she needed to learn his body. Besides, if his instincts about her experience or lack thereof were right, she needed all the time and encouragement he could give her. He steeled himself for more of her touch.

She became bolder, first, with slipping more of her hand inside the material, then finally dragging the sweats down, letting them settle around his ankles. Quickly stepping out of the puddled material, he stood nude for her viewing pleasure.

Her eyes widened then she licked her lips. Appreciation flashed across her face along with a healthy dose of curiosity, awe, and sensual longing.

A balm to his soul and an aphrodisiac more potent than any pill could ever be.

As much as he enjoyed her open exploration of his flesh, he needed to turn the tables and focus on her. Right now, it was his turn to learn more about his lover. He grabbed her hand as she reached out to touch his erection. "Later."

Bewilderment crossed her face.

"I need to touch you." With that said, he made short work of her sweatshirt, leaving her upper body bare. Raspberry nipples ripe for the taking stood out from modest but perky breasts. Nowhere near average—beautiful and perfect and his.

"Kiss you." Leaning in, he brushed his tongue across one side, before taking the nub fully into his mouth, sucking gently.

Lily gasped and stumbled slightly under his tender assault.

Upon bending down, he swept her legs up, cradling her against his chest, until he reached the bed. He laid her down near the center, pausing a moment to take in her beautiful body. Faint bristle marks gave one breast a rosy tint compared to the other. Her flat belly quivered with her erratic breaths.

Cale slid one knee on the bed, reaching down to snag her sweatpants, giving them a tug.

Lily lifted her hips, allowing for easy removal, leaving her clad only in a pair of small pink cotton panties that accented more than they distracted.

Sucking his breath in at the vision before him, Cale settled alongside her, his hands automatically seeking those glorious breasts he'd recently discovered. He kissed her long and hard before pulling away to lick down her neck, slowly edging downwards. Laving his tongue over the closest breast, he nuzzled and suckled, before moving to its twin, greeting it with the same eager abandon. The peaks grew taut under his affections as she wrapped her arms around him and pulled him closer, communicating her need for more of the same.

Lily arched up beneath his ministrations, her body clamoring for more, even as her breathing escalated. He could almost hear her heart speed beneath that exquisite chest. Pride and satisfaction surged through him at her delightful responses.

He edged south, swirling around her navel before tracing down to rest squarely between her legs.

Her legs clamped together, trapping his hand between them, as she sucked in air. Tension radiated over her small frame.

Lifting from his feast on her breasts, he stared down into her face, reading her expression with ease.

Her half-lidded bedroom eyes spoke of the sensual spell she was under with her blatant enjoyment of his touch—if the wetness on her panties was any indication. She met his gaze as her teeth worried her lip—a sure sign of nerves and perhaps a hint of indecision. Considering her untried status, he expected some cautionary reflexes on her part.

"Easy." *Knee-jerk reaction.* He would bet on it. "I'm not going to hurt you."

"I know. I'm sorry. I just..." She glanced away, a flush covering her face.

"Just?" he pressed her, leaving a trail of kisses from her shoulder back to one delectable breast.

"I haven't..."

Cale rested his weight on one elbow. "Lily, look at me."

She complied, her eyes wide and expressive.

"Virgin?" he whispered the words, then twisted his trapped hand slightly, encouraging her to make room by relaxing her legs.

Scarlet color flamed across her face as she turned away. "Yes."

He barely heard the whispered admission. Not that it surprised him, considering her shy responses thus far. Hell, he'd pretty much labeled her untouched back on day one. Her actions and those pink cheeks had told the story.

Cale nipped her collarbone, bringing her attention back to him. The need to comfort her, coax her, and allow her to see through his eyes prodded him to offer up his inner thoughts. "Do you know how special you are?" He followed it with a lick across a tasty nipple. "Beautiful and sexy, a siren." He had never been a man for flattery and lots of flowery words in bed. But, then again, he had never bedded a virgin before. All his playmates had been well experienced and needed little encouragement and direction. *Until Lily.* Something deep down clenched at the thought of being her first. *And only.* The thought startled him. But, the more he considered it, the more it felt right. He would make sure her first time proved memorable because of the wonderful sensations and erotic happenings, a standard for all other encounters to compare to.

Armed with knowledge and resolution, Cale continued his explorations, kissing trails over her body, all the while working over her core, getting her used to his gentle touches in such a sensitive area. Within minutes, she opened her legs, allowing him greater access, not voicing a single complaint when he hooked his thumbs under the cotton and slowly removed her last remaining garment. He soaked up the sight of her naked on the bed before him, blonde hair spilled on the coverlet, as she shifted her legs apart once more, exposing her glistening pink folds covered by a sparse collection of light brown curls. His cock jerked as he puffed out a breath of air at the sheer beauty before him. As much as he wanted to cover her and sink into her depths, he paused to commit this picture to memory.

"Cale?" Her raspy voice jerked him into action.

"I'm right here." He slid from the bed and marched to his discarded pants. After taking a condom out of his wallet, he returned to her side, planting kisses across her tummy in apology for making her wait.

Lily reached down, bracketed his head with her hands, and pulled him upwards, pressing her lips against his. Her tongue initiated the connection, slipping into his mouth, raking over his teeth, and flicking against his own, in an age-old game of tag.

He kissed her deeply and passionately, distracting her while he sought the damp depths of her femininity once more. Ever so slowly, he parted the flesh, sliding easily in the moisture until he found the nubbin he sought. With practiced ease, he raked one finger lightly over the top, then circled the area.

A low groan sounded from Lily's throat. Lily arched into his hand, reacting to his caress. Her arms wrapped around his neck, as if she were afraid of falling if she didn't wrap him up tight. He felt as much as heard her gasp.

Satisfaction spread over him at her untried and shy responses. His gut clenched as his cock throbbed with need. *Patience.* He wasn't a small man. And no way in hell would he hurt her.

Cale worked the area a little longer, drawing more wetness. He lowered his mouth to her neck, licking across her pulse, as below he gently but steadily pushed one finger into her depths.

Coated walls clasped him tightly, more so as Lily writhed under his invasion. Rather than shifting away, she lifted closer. Giving her a moment to adjust, Cale retreated only to return again, more insistent and heading deeper as his thumb swirled in a lazy circle around her clit.

"Oh, yes. Please. More." She spoke between pants as she reached out to pull at his shoulders.

Cale doubled his presence inside her, focusing on her face for any signs of discomfort. He saw none, only growing arousal and need.

The throbbing discomfort in his leaking dick grew unbearable, snapping his tightly held control. Quickly, he removed his hand to tear open the packet on the bed. In a flash, he rolled the condom into place, and once again looked down at Lily.

She opened her eyes to meet his.

Holding her gaze, he lowered his larger frame over hers, careful to keep most of his weight on his forearms. He kissed her softly as she rubbed and massaged his back, holding him close while she returned his kisses enthusiastically.

Upon lining up his hips, he pressed the head of his erection against her, pushing slowly and gently. Her body parted for him, welcoming him back with greater tightness and more liquid than before. Languidly, he made his first entry, pushing past the initial resistance of her core. Her breath hitched at his slight invasion. He waited a beat, licked her throat, then continued, his senses open to her every response, observing her body language for any hint of discomfort.

Moving unhurriedly, he bore down until he felt her flinch under him. Feeling and understanding why, he paused once more. "Lily? Look at me, sugar."

She turned, opened her eyelids, allowing those pretty hazel eyes to meet his. Her chest heaved with rapid breaths as she held onto his sides, as if bracing for a hard impact.

"You sure?" He gave her one final opportunity to escape, her virginity intact.

"Yes. I want this. You." She held his gaze steadily. The earlier hesitation gone.

The words opened something deep inside. No way could he leave her now. Instead, he focused on getting past the obstruction with the least amount of pain possible. Sealing his lips over hers, he thrust powerfully, punching through the frail barrier with finesse and precision.

She sucked in a breath, her body jerking in an instinctive retreat. Muscles tensed and locked tight, holding him in place deep inside her body as she gripped his shoulders, nails digging into flesh for a purchase.

Cale remained still, soothing her with soft kisses and whispered endearments, apologizing for causing her even the slightest pang while praising her efforts and beauty. He licked, he nibbled, he showered her with every ounce of affection possible, needing for her to open her eyes, reassure him the worst had passed, and allow him to lead her to sweet heaven.

Muscle by muscle, Lily relaxed under him. She sighed softly, her hold on him lightening by the second even as her hips began to lift, tentatively at first, then with more zest.

Taking the hint, Cale began to ease back a little before pressing in once more. The tightness remained, which tested his willpower greatly. He shoved his immense need aside, determined for Lily to find her pleasure first. Nothing mattered more than Lily's pleasure, her climax, her happiness in their union.

He reached down where their bodies met, searching until he found the tight nubbin, stroking it in rhythm with his movements. Circling the sensitive flesh, he brushed her clit before plucking tenderly.

She cried out and set her sharp teeth against his shoulder. The nip threw accelerant on his already raging desire.

Stubbornly, he stuck to the course, slow movements that pulled him nearly free of her channel, then returning to seek her very depths once more. In. Out. He sucked in air and refused to sprint, holding steady instead. A snail's pace, true, but still highly stimulating. Her snug body fit him, massaging his thick and full member, heating his blood to a fever pitch. Dampness increased as he rocked with exquisite care, testing her ability to take his fullness while plundering her body for hotspots to drive her insane with need. Over and over, he moved, driving them both toward the pinnacle with gentle strokes designed to feed her hunger and whet her desire for more.

Lily released him as she gripped the sheets so hard her knuckles turned white. She opened her mouth and turned her head this way and that. A whimper of sheer need escaped from her throat.

Tingling began at the base of his spine, signaling his upcoming release.

Pulling on all his reserves, Cale ground his teeth as his fingers flew over her burgeoning flesh, pressing a bit harder, while he sought the deepest penetration possible.

Lily arched her hips off the bed and threw her head back on a muted whimper. A grimace of sexual completion covered her face as a crimson flush spread quickly over her face, neck, and chest. Strong contractions squeezed his cock, sending him over the edge with a gruff shout.

Spasms raced through his body, fiery pulses of ecstasy. He crested hard, the sensations so powerful he could have sworn he'd found the all elusive perfect moment in life. Wave after wave followed as he gyrated against her body, reluctant to do more than soak up the rapture as her strong walls milked him for every drop of cum he possessed. Finally, totally spent, he rested on top of her, sated for the time being.

Lily's body still pulsed now and again with each small shift in their position. Her breathing slowed before she finally opened her eyes.

He pushed upwards, removing some of his weight from her slighter frame while he watched her closely, trying to read the thoughts obviously filling her mind. "Are you okay?" His entry had hurt her, he knew that. She'd also climaxed under him. That feather he stuffed in his hat proudly.

"Yes. That was...surprising."

Surprising? What the hell does that mean? He kicked himself, realizing he sounded like a teenager, questioning and rating his sexual performance. "That's good, right?"

A soft expression covered her face. She reached up, wrapped her arms around his neck, and pulled him down for a soft kiss. "It was better than good. Wonderful, in fact."

His ego expanded with the praise. Returning the quick kiss, he untangled her arms. "Hold on."

Retreating gently, he eased himself from her body, holding onto the condom as he did so. She twitched from the motion, but quickly relaxed once he had exited fully.

He pulled off the condom, tied it up, and headed to the bathroom to dispose of it. While in there, he found a washcloth under the sink and wet it with warm water. After cleansing himself, he washed the linen back out, then strode back to the bed, his gaze raking over Lily the entire way. *Beautiful.* The pink tint on her skin only added to the classical curves. Her chest expanded, drawing attention to her cherry tipped breasts, still pebbled from his attentions and their play. She radiated beauty and more. He found her exceptional, unique, and damn alluring.

Sitting on the bed, he lifted the warm cloth above the junction of her thighs. Her face flamed as she wiggled. He read her embarrassment easily. In time, he knew she would become accustomed to his touch and attentions. Today, he gave her the first taste of passion. The first of many to come, he vowed.

Trailing his fingers up her inner thigh, he coaxed her legs apart once more.

"I can do it. I'll get up and…"

Cale shook his head. "Shhh. Let me." The intimacy of his intentions struck a chord as he considered her shyness and newness to a man's touch. Never before had she let a man caress her sweet body. Cale changed that. The significance moved him and intensified his possessive desire to keep her at his side.

He set about his task as matter-of-factly as possible, caring for her like an everyday occurrence. Tenderly, he cleansed the area, noting the few splotches of blood on the soft material. The condom had borne the same speckled appearance.

He remained quiet, the implications of his actions settling on his shoulders. She'd given herself to him. He'd be damned if he turned his back and dashed off, abandoning her like a common streetwalker. No. While his future remained up in the air, he knew Lily would hold her own spot, a priority ranking.

She turned her head, but didn't offer further protests.

He finished the chore, tossed the cloth into the hamper, and returned to her side. After, sliding his arms around her, he pulled her close.

Thoughts raced through his head as he kissed her shoulder and neck, not wanting to excite, but more to soothe and share. *Cuddle.* Never before had he wanted to snuggle with a woman after sex. If pressured, he did so reluctantly, counting the seconds until he could leave without having to deal with an avalanche of tears and anger. Lily made it different. He wanted to stay with her, hold her close. Protect her from any harm.

Something about her called to him on a basic level. *Her innocence?* He considered that for a few beats before giving the equivalent of a mental shrug. That certainly was part of it, but there was more. He felt deeper about her than anyone else. *Love?*

Lily turned to rest on her back, looking up at him with those expressive eyes. She wore the smug look of a woman well-loved and fast coming into her own.

She took one of his hands, then pulled it to her mouth, planting kisses to the palm. Her gaze never wavered while she used her other hand to trace down his side, tickling his loin, before wrapping around his flesh. It jerked with her inquisitive caresses. "Is it finally my turn to touch again?" An impish smile shaped her lips in an upward arch.

He enjoyed her teasing more than he cared to admit. "You do know where that will lead?"

"Oh, yes," she whispered as she nipped his thumb with her teeth. "Magical places."

Magical places indeed.

Chapter Seventeen

Lily woke slowly, warm inside a cocoon of blankets with strong arms wrapped around her, a muscular chest providing a cushion to her back. Her mind quickly recapped last night's events, causing her stomach to clench and summersault. She certainly couldn't complain. What had Cale said before? It was all in the preparation? That might be true, but she had a hunch it was the man himself that deserved most of the credit.

He trailed his hand from her belly, heading north until it cupped a naked, full breast. She sucked in a breath with the gentle tightening of his fingers as he revisited territory he'd explored thoroughly before.

After turning over, she rested on her side, looking down at Cale as he lay on his back. Uncertainty flared, her courage fleeing as she gazed down into his face. *What if he regrets what we did? It's not like I'm anywhere near the class of women he's used to.*

He lightly stroked her back with long fingers, watching her face carefully. "Good morning."

"Morning." Unsure what else to say, she remained mute, waiting for the other boot to drop.

Charity took that moment to climb up the side of the bed, heading straight for Cale's chest. She plopped down smack dab in the middle of his sternum, staring at him as if willing him to understand and obey. A second later, she leaned over, sinking her teeth into his nipple.

"Ow. Damn." Cale grabbed her in both hands, lifted her up, and met her eye for eye. "First of all, that's not gonna get you any milk and secondly, it's no wonder your mother is trying to wean you. Those teeth are like daggers."

Lily burst out laughing, clutching the blanket while holding her belly. All the tension of the morning began to ease away. Leave it to Charity, the troublemaker, to decide Cale made a good substitute mother.

Cale shook his head, setting the kitten against Lily's arm. Charity immediately looked up at her, then down to her chest. "Oh, no. Don't look at me. I'm of no more help than he is."

Shooting them both a look of disdain and total disgust, Charity leaped off the bed and walked out of the bedroom, tail high in the air.

Cale snorted, but broke his tough guy persona with soft laughter at such dramatic antics as he absently rubbed the injured area.

Lily's heart soared as she joined him with giggles. "Want me to kiss it and make it better?" The whispered words teased as she coyly peeked through her lashes.

His eyes became heavy-lidded, something sultry sparking in those depths as the corners of his mouth kicked up. "Nurses are supposed to ease suffering, after all." Giving his nipple one more brush, he sighed dramatically. "And, oh, am I suffering."

She snorted. Shakespeare he would never be. But his light jovial manner mixed with innuendoes kept happiness flowing through her, giving her energy, and joy in life, and in the man she loved.

Upon leaning over, she flicked her tongue slowly across his nipple, earning a low groan for her efforts. "There. All better now."

He pouted like a small boy being told homework came before playing baseball with his buddies.

She sat up, pulling the blanket with her, after tapping his lips with her finger.

"Where are you going?" His face quickly turned to an expression of concern while he grabbed her hips, holding her still.

"To feed the bottomless pits, of course. I would hate for Charity to return and bite something else if she doesn't get her breakfast." Sending him a smile full of promises, she climbed off him and out of the bed.

"Good point." Cale reclined back, folding his hands under his head, watching her every move. "Why are you taking the blanket?"

She didn't stop to answer. "It's cold and... Well, it's cold." Her face heated even as she left the room on her way to the kitchen to feed the girls followed by a quick stop in the spare bathroom to make herself presentable. It wasn't every day she slept with a man and ran around the house naked. Last night had been a first for the former and she didn't think she could quite muster the latter.

As it was, each step drew her attention to the soreness between her legs, reminding her of the passion they'd shared. She had no regrets and couldn't have found a better man to be with. *That doesn't mean he feels the same way.* Pushing that thought aside, she focused on the moment, buying time before she had that discussion with him.

She caught a glimpse of Cale's discarded T-shirt lying on the floor from the night before. Without a second thought, she snatched it up and pulled it over her head, dropping the blanket as she did so. The borrowed garment fell to mid-thigh. More comfortable now that she was covered, Lily tossed the blanket on the couch, and headed into the kitchen.

A few minutes later, she returned to the bedroom. He probably wouldn't complain about bed head or bad morning breath, but she couldn't help being self-conscious.

Her breath caught at the sight of Cale lying on his side, chin resting on his palm, as his gaze tracked her movements. Sparks flared in those light blue eyes. The corners of his mouth tilted upwards as he patted the mattress beside him.

Obediently, she climbed back into the bed, ignoring the twinge of discomfort the action caused. She needed his reassurance at the moment and cuddling was a nice start. She could easily become addicted to Cale wrapped around her, keeping her warm and secure, pampering her like a cherished treasure.

"Feeling shy this morning?" When she drew close enough, he reached out, sliding one hand under his borrowed T-shirt to cup her bare rear.

"Some." She scurried into place, making sure all her essential parts were covered. Not that she expected such a thin barrier to deter Cale.

He tucked her against him, positioning her on her back, while he remained on his side. Not bothering with the covers, he sprinkled tender kisses over her forehead and nose. "Now, where were we?" The low sultry tone promised another lesson in making love.

"Sleeping?"

The corners of his mouth kicked up. "Hmmm." He trailed kisses down her neck only to latch onto her breast after he fisted the shirt and tugged it out of the way. "Maybe just about here."

Lily bit back a moan, shifting closer to his talented mouth. Never would she have dreamed it could be like this. Sensations of burning fire splashed through her blood, settling in the pit of her stomach. The heat made her ache for more.

His hand roamed lower to cup her femininity. "Sore?"

She couldn't quite meet his gaze, but managed to nod. Having sex was a heck of a lot easier to do than talk about. At this rate it would take a mere half century for her to stop blushing at every little thing.

Cale released a sigh before locking her tightly in his arms. "I'm sorry."

She gave him a small smile. "I'm not. I never imagined it would be like that."

"Like how?" He rubbed her tummy gently.

"Like, with you, I could actually fly." She cupped his cheek, placing a tender kiss to his lips. "I do want you."

"And you'll have me. Later." He tapped her nose with a finger then kissed the same area. "Maybe after a long hot soak in the tub."

"Promise?" Reaching around, she rubbed and massaged his lower back with one hand, unable to resist touching his glorious body, thrilled in the ability to finally experience skin to skin contact with this man.

"Promise," he whispered against her ear as he nibbled on the lobe.

"I love you, Cale," she muttered softly against his ear, flicking her tongue across it to seal the deal.

Cale jerked his head up, intensely searching her face.

Throwing caution to the wind, Lily said it again. Louder. "I love you."

He sat up and finger-combed his hair with one hand. All the while not saying a word.

Lily's heart plummeted. *It's okay. I love him enough for both of us.* The thought didn't re-form the bubble of optimism that burst with his wordless reaction. "It's… I…" What was she supposed to say now? She could hardly take it back. But, at the same time, she felt idiotic spilling her innermost feelings to someone who obviously didn't return those same sentiments.

"This is harder than I thought," Cale sighed.

The pained expression made her feel even worse. Her comment had turned a magical morning into one full of awkwardness. She edged away after flipping over, intent upon escape now that the spell had broken.

Cale refused to let her go. His hand snagged around her middle, pulling her flush against his front. "Wait. Please." He brushed stray hairs off her face. "I need to explain."

Lily tilted to get comfortable. Her gaze never left his face as she waited for him to speak.

He pulled in a deep breath. "I need to tell you about my ex-wife. Beautiful as the day is long, but shallow and cold-hearted underneath." He nuzzled her cheek. "Everyone tried to tell me, but I refused to listen. Instead, she led me around by my dumb handle, spending every penny I could make on expensive baubles, complaining how she didn't like being left alone while I was away on missions, and demanding more of everything." He paused a second before continuing. "She ended up driving a wedge between my parents and me with her selfish nature and my blindness to her true self."

Lily's heart broke for Cale, knowing he suffered far worse than he let on. She rubbed her hand over his, offering quiet support as he finished his explanation.

"One day Dillon and I came home early from a mission. Excited to see her again, we drove straight to my apartment. I found her in our bed with another man." His tone sharpened as if he relived the betrayal.

"I'm so sorry. I don't understand how anyone could do that to you."

His eyes darkened with emotion. "I was beyond pissed. Probably could have killed them both with my bare hands in that moment. I vented. She fired right back, blaming me for her cheating."

"That witch. How could she?" Lily's temper began to rise, only able to imagine what Cale must have felt at that moment.

"She cited my absence, my inability to please her, my lack of riches. She threw everything in my face."

"What did you do?" The words came out softly.

"I walked away before I did something really stupid. Filed for divorce the next day."

"I'm sure that wasn't easy."

"No, but neither was the divorce. She fought tooth and nail for everything."

Lily reached up and cupped his cheek. "At least you're free of her barnacle tendrils and nastiness. But, I'm still sorry. I can't imagine."

Suddenly, so many things made perfect sense to her — Cale's attitude, his lack of trust, his reluctance to her initial offer of friendship. The man had had his heart shredded by one evil woman. No wonder he pulled back into himself and forgot how to enjoy the small gifts and blessings in life.

"It killed something inside me." Regret and resolution laced his tone as if the statement had been forcibly dragged from the recesses of his heart.

The admission cost him, she easily read between the lines. He opened himself up to her, showed his vulnerability, and trusted her with not only his story, but so much more.

She developed an instant hate for his ex. How could anyone do such a thing? Especially to Cale. He did nothing but care for others, putting his life on the line day in and day out to keep the world safe. He didn't deserve such betrayal. No one did.

His explanation made her realize something else. She didn't need to hear the words. His actions told her all she needed to know. No man could have been more understanding or gentle with her. Protective and kind. The words may never come, but she had her answer in each kiss, each caress, and every moment of pleasure he rained upon her. It may not be love, but it was in the same ballpark in her book.

Lily brushed her thumb over his five o'clock shadow, enjoying the slightly prickly sensation. "I'm sorry. I wish I had something better to say to take away all the pain."

He nuzzled her palm. "I know."

"I still love you." She smiled up at him.

Relief and amusement flashed across his face, replacing strain and sorrow. "I—"

She covered his lips with a finger, sealing in whatever he was going to say. "It's okay. You don't have to say the words. In fact, I would prefer you don't unless you really mean it and are comfortable saying it." She replaced the finger with her lips, softly meshing hers with his.

He responded in kind, gentle and lazy.

I could wake up every morning to this.

Cale broke off the kiss. He gripped her shoulders and lightly rubbed. "We should stop before I get carried away."

Lily nodded. *Later.* She could wait a bit longer.

For his love, she could wait a lifetime.

Chapter Eighteen

Lily walked across the room with nothing more than a towel wrapped around her slender body. Her still damp hair hung straight down her back, the slight waviness more pronounced than usual. As Cale watched from the couch a droplet of water dripped down her chest, between her beautiful breasts, only to be absorbed into the terry cloth towel.

His cock hardened instantly.

If he didn't catch her, she would duck into the bedroom and pull on her clothes, covering the body he hungered for like a man on a week-long trip through the desert. "Lily?"

She paused, spun around and faced him. Hazel eyes sparked, then turned the slightest bit smoky. He read intent and want in her face.

They'd spent the rest of the morning with her chores, playing with the kittens, and fixing a meal. He'd bided his time, allowing her ample time to recover from her first sexual experience, determined not to rush her into the next round. Yet, afternoon had arrived and he could no more keep his hands off her than he could control the planetary alignment. "Come here." The soft command carried more than a subtle hint at his intentions. He patted his lap.

A small simper appeared on her face, promising mischief. "Is there something you want?" She ambled over, standing before him, a thick towel the only barrier between him and her naked flesh.

"Oh, yeah. You. I want you." He stared up at her as she processed his words. He reached out, bracketed her hips and gave them a squeeze.

"Hmmm."

He arched an eyebrow, recognizing her attempts at lighthearted teasing. "What does 'hmmm' mean?"

Still gripping the towel tightly, she raked her gaze over his body. A grin followed. "I didn't get to finish touching your body last time."

His libido rocketed at the very thought of her hands running over him, leaving small fires in their wake. He couldn't last long enough to sate her curiosity, wasn't sure he could this time, either. But he'd give it his best shot.

He stood up and started peeling clothes with practiced ease, tossing each garment into a pile on the floor, watching her face the entire time. Appreciation and awe broadcast loudly as she licked her lips and focused on his revealed skin. Finally naked, he stood up straight. Holding his arms out, he grinned. "I'm all yours for the taking."

Almost hesitantly, she stepped closer, trailing her fingers down his sternum and over his abs. The skin twitched under her tender foray and cranked up the heat all the more.

Damn. Just a touch from this woman and he fired on all cylinders. The fact would rattle him to the core and slam up his defensive barriers if he didn't see and understand Lily's gift—her goodness, humanity, and love.

"So strong. Powerful." She whispered her findings. "Gorgeous."

He fisted his hands in an attempt to hold still, allowing her to learn his body as he'd learned hers last night. "I'm battle scarred and hard."

Lily tilted her head, meeting his gaze for a split second before looking down. "Scars add character." She wrapped her fingers around his cock, sending a surge of desire boiling in his veins. "Definitely hard, though."

He bit back a groan as she measured him in a steamy caress.

"So big. I still can't believe you fit inside me."

Her naive statement nearly broke his resolve. Through narrowed eyelids, he watched as she stroked him with open curiosity before dropping lower to discover another elemental difference between men and women. She cupped his sac, then rolled his balls as if weighing the orbs. "So soft."

"You're driving me insane." He gritted out the words. Her gentle stroking made his erection ache, swell even more, and send a flurry of pleasure through him. At this rate, he wouldn't last too much longer.

For a moment he considered giving in, letting her jack him off, watching the surprise on her face as he shot a load all over her towel.

"You like that, don't you?" She gripped his dick with more confidence, brushing her thumb over the sensitive tip. Before he could answer, she continued, "I think you do since there's moisture leaking out."

She collected the bead on her finger then brought it to her lips. Licking, she appeared to decide if she enjoyed the small flavor or not. "Tangy." Her eyes met his. "Can I taste you?"

The request knocked him off balance. He blew out a breath and nodded. "Anything you want, sugar. I'm all yours." While running his fingers through her hair, he positioned her head for his kiss. Leaning in, he slowly meshed their lips, flicked his tongue over the seam, then dove in when she opened for him. He plundered deep, leaving no area untouched. She mirrored his actions, though less aggressively. Their tongues tapped, wrestled, and finally broke apart.

He wanted nothing more than to lay her down and glide into her wet, hot channel, but that would wait. First came her wishes. The only unresolved question remained how she wanted to do this.

Sitting back down on the couch, he met her gaze. "Where do you want me?"

She tapped her finger on her lips. "Just like that. I want to watch your face so I know if I'm doing it right."

"Sweetheart, there's no doing it wrong." Leaning back against the couch, he spread his legs and waited.

Lily lowered to her knees, then scooted forward until she knelt between his thighs. After once more grabbing his cock, she lifted the thick tool to her lips, then licked across the tip.

Cale jerked as delicious flames spread across his groin. He gritted his teeth and braced himself for more.

After a couple more tests, Lily grew bolder. She opened wide and took the entire head in her mouth, closed down, and sucked. Her gaze lifted to his.

He groaned, placed a hand on the top of her head, and resisted the urge to thrust against her. "That's it. Just like that. Feels so good." He offered the words of encouragement in an almost growl as he sucked in air and grappled with his unsteady control.

She dropped the towel, freeing her other hand to rediscover his balls. She lashed her tongue down his length, and squeezed with her fingers as she played with his most sensitive area with inquisitive gentleness. The forces combined in a fiery passion so hot his entire world centered on Lily's ministrations and his fast approaching climax.

"Fuck." His hips hunched as he teetered on the pinnacle.

Lily took more of his throbbing erection in her mouth then purred as she ran her tongue frantically over his flesh.

The vibrations sent him right to the very edge. "I'm going to come." He bit out the words a second before his prediction proved true. His lower body tightened, then exploded as the tides of rapture cascaded over him in spicy rhythm. He shivered as he rocketed to nirvana in a heartbeat.

Her actions never stopped, not even when the first pulse of semen left his body and sprayed her mouth. She bobbed, she licked, she sucked, and swallowed. Never once did she cringe or push him away. Instead, she asked for more as if his essence could provide life-sustaining nourishment.

Panting, he petted her hair, easing her off his slowly deflating cock. Her tongue gathered up one more drop before she sat back on her heels, a look of satisfaction on her face. "Tastes like chicken."

Laughter came out of nowhere. He let loose with deep belly guffaws before subsiding to chuckles. He couldn't remember ever having this much fun during sex before. Lily. She made it all new.

"Is that so?"

"Yep." Her towel slipped down to her waist, leaving her pretty breasts bare.

His arousal returned with a vengeance. "Then let's see what you taste like." He scooped her up off the floor and laid her down on the couch sans towel. Once she adjusted herself he covered her body, kissing her for long minutes before trailing nibbles and kisses down her neck and chest, paying particular attention to her breasts. He couldn't get enough of those perky orbs and their delicious raspberry peaks. Only when she writhed under him and both nipples stood at attention did he resume his journey.

Shifting back, he placed his hands on her inner thighs, thrilled at the lack of protest as he neared her secret place. "Open for me, sugar."

She parted her legs, but not near enough. The couch didn't allow for as much room as he'd hoped for. Not to be deterred, he lifted her right leg and hooked her heel over the back of the sofa. The other leg, he nudged until her foot rested on the ground.

Uncertainty flared in her face for a moment. "Cale…"

"Shh." He bent over until his nose bumped her outer lips. "Let me taste you just like you tasted me."

Dipping a finger into her core, he met an abundance of moisture, heat, and a snug ring of muscles that welcomed him back. "Damn, you're wet. Sucking me off turned you on."

She whimpered in answer. The implicit trust in her response clicked with something deep inside.

He pulled back, added in a second digit, then pushed back inside. Once there, he ran his tongue along the edge of her inner lips, lapping up her juices. Intoxicating. Delicious. Perfect. He licked, he fingered her, he savored every cry he wrung from her throat.

Nuzzling her clit, he spared a moment to glance up.

Lily lay spread out, her chest heaving, her fists clenched in the pillow under her head. Eyes closed, her taut features told him she lay on a rack of intense pleasure. The sight stimulated him all the more.

With exquisite precision, he traced her clit, then licked over the sensitive nubbin.

She jerked and groaned, yet held her position. Again, he repeated the caress before sealing his lips over the area and sucking.

Lily cried out, her pelvis lifting to meet him. "Please. Oh, Cale. Please."

He released her button for a second. "Please what?"

She opened her eyes—the smoldering look said it all. "Please make love to me."

Initially, he wanted to make her come just like this. To repay her gift to him. However, he couldn't deny this latest invitation, not when he wanted her so badly. He'd go down on her again later. After all, they had two more days before she returned to work— plenty of time to dip into both of their libraries of fantasies. By Monday, they would know one another's body as well as they knew their own.

Cale helped her to sit up, taking advantage of the closeness to run the tip of his tongue up her neck and over to her earlobe. He worried the area for a moment before stepping back to find his pants. After digging for a second, he plucked his wallet out, dug out a condom, then quickly rolled the rubber on. Catching her staring, he grinned wickedly before sitting back on the couch properly once more. "I want you to ride me."

Her hazel eyes flared.

He saw the excitement and interest written clearly on her face. She might be one step from virginity, but she had already blossomed under his tutelage.

After snagging her hand, he pulled her to him, assisting her to straddle his hips. She sat on his thighs, legs spread, and grasped his shoulders for balance.

The erotic position drew attention to her moist, pink folds. He lightly brushed his fingers over her mound and dipped inside. Her body tightened immediately, a reaction he couldn't wait to experience on his cock buried in her perfect core.

Grasping her hip with one hand, he wrapped the other around his erection, lined up their bodies, and nestled the tip of his swollen member against her entrance. "Sink down, Lily."

She complied, lowering her body by tiny increments, the motion both teasing and torture at the same time.

He sucked in a breath and savored every ripple of her delicate flesh, every catch in her breathing, every tiny mew from her throat. More than once he had to remind himself of her naivety and the need for patience and tenderness owing to his arousal at an all-time fevered pitch. He couldn't remember ever wanting a woman as much as he wanted Lily.

A soft grunt sounded as she descended the last couple of inches. Her nails bit into the skin at his shoulders, the small sting only adding to his inferno of raging desire. "That's it, sugar." He watched her face closely, noting the furrow to her brow as well as the spark in her eyes — all testament to the myriad of sensations coursing through her body.

He wrapped his arms around her waist then latched onto a rosy-tipped nipple directly in front of his face. Laving and sucking, he pulled the nubbin taut before turning to shower the other breast with similar affection. Then he took more of the orb into his mouth, savoring the taste.

"Oh, Cale." Lily began to move, at first a rocking motion, then lifting slightly before dropping back down. Each almost tentative wiggle clenched her inner muscles, rubbed his cock in all the right places, and sprinkled him with more feminine juices.

He allowed the breast to pop out of his mouth. "Ride me, Lily. Take all you need, just don't stop." A groan escaped his lips as she did as bidden.

With more confidence, she gyrated, bounced, and wiggled her hips, sending cascades of pleasure surging through his body. She'd picked up on the rhythm quickly and now embraced the actions wholeheartedly. She opened her mouth, tilted her head back, and she cupped the back of his head, her fingers lacing through his hair as her pace picked up.

Bracketing her hips once more, he steadied her in her hard gallop to the finish. Unable to help himself, he began to meet her strokes, tightening his rear in order to press every bit of his cock to the very deepest point possible.

"I need…" She began to pant.

He knew exactly what she needed. A little help in reaching her goal.

Deftly, he slipped his hand between their bodies, found the place where they joined, then headed north a smidgen. He circled her clit, moving ever closer, before blatantly brushing his thumb over.

She jerked and slammed down against him with a cry.

Smiling like a wolf, he repeated the caress, feeling her body tense under his arm. Unrepentantly, he fiddled with her nub and tightened his hold.

"Cale. Please." Her breasts rubbed against his chest as she leaned into his body, her pelvis rolling and humping in an effort to find the exact spot.

He nibbled on a bouncing breast and pressed harder on her bundle of nerves with his thumb.

Tight as a bowstring, she quivered. He plucked the area twice, then massaged with precise pressure, not letting up in the least, no matter her frantic movements.

The walls of her core clamped down like a vice just before rhythmic contractions lapped at his deeply buried erection like a dozen tongues striving to coat him with hot cream. She yelped as her muscles continued to massage him with surprising strength, fast-tracking him straight to the very peak.

He released her flesh, looked into her scrunched up face, and followed her straight into rapture.

For several minutes, only the sounds of their breathing broke the silence of the room as he tried to catch his breath. Cale nuzzled Lily's chest, fully sated and content to savor the after-sex glow with her still locked in his arms. *Where she belongs.*

The once heart-stuttering thought no longer set off a flight or fight reaction. Instead, warmth soaked through to his very soul.

Together they sparked a passion so hot and intimate, Cale knew the figurative chains of desire would keep them locked together, no matter how far the physical distance. With such a strong attachment in place, he would return to her again. Nothing could keep him away.

Chapter Nineteen

The phone chimed, pulling Cale from his devious thoughts of Lily finishing her shower. They'd spent the entire day before learning one another's body. Today, he planned to take her out to eat on what could be called their official first date.

He grinned to himself at the irony as he answered the call. "Yeah?"

"Shit, Cale. Can't you say 'hello' like the rest of the world?"

Cale rolled his eyes. Dillon found any excuse to yank his chain. He'd play along—after all, this morning was proving bright and pretty damn cheerful. "Hello, Dillon. How's it hanging in your neck of the woods?"

"Damn good."

"Della taking care of you?" Cale already knew the answer, but asked anyway.

"Oh, yeah. Excellent care."

"Uh-huh." He could easily read between the lines. "As long as you're getting proper exercise."

"Count on it." Dillon's tone carried happiness. Della did that for him. A better woman couldn't be found for Dillon in Cale's opinion. Cale had his own gem in the form of Lily.

"How's Lily?" Dillon asked.

Cale pondered how much to admit to his younger brother. "She's fine."

"Just fine? Because I saw the looks you gave one another. The sweet kisses. She's got your number, bro."

Cale blew out a breath and answered truthfully. "Yeah, she does."

"Ah-ha. I knew it." Dillon chuckled. "Sounds like both of you are smitten and something tells me you've spent more than your fair share of time in bed."

"Not going there." Cale drew a hard line in the sand. He really didn't want to discuss his love life with Dillon. Not now, probably not ever.

"That bad, huh?" Dillon needled him.

"More like that good." He corrected Dillon's way of thinking. "I just never thought I would find a woman to be with like her."

Dillon paused for a moment before asking. "Think Lily is the one?"

"If she isn't, then I don't know who is." Cale verbalized the words he'd only spoken inside his mind so far.

"A little scary? Troubling?"

"I believe in Lily, but—"

"You can't help but wonder if there's another knife about to be plunged in your back?"

"Yeah." Cale ran a hand through his hair. He promised himself to take one day at a time, let a relationship evolve. No rushing, no putting the cart before the horse.

He snorted to himself. *Like you're already done in taking her out on the town for the first time after taking her to bed. Taking her in the bed. On the couch.*

"Cale?"

Dillon's voice pulled him back to the conversation at hand. "Still here."

"I don't know much…"

"Now that's the damn truth."

"But, the way I see it, Lily's special. Hell, if you don't believe me, wait until you ship off on another mission. If you miss her, think of her, and can't wait to rush home, there might be your answer."

Cale considered his brother's advice and the statement rang true. "You might have something there."

"How do you think I knew for sure about Della?"

"She had you walking around with a hard-on all the time?" Cale grinned, enjoying aggravating Dillon.

"Never knew you were busy checking out my crotch. Must go hand in hand with that ladies underwear fetish you have." Teasing entered Dillon's voice.

"Is there a reason you called besides to harass me this morning?"

"Just making sure you didn't traumatize the poor girl."

"Cale? I'll be ready in a couple of minutes. Just have to get the cats fed," Lily called from the back room.

"Take your time."

Dillon laughed. "Doesn't sound traumatized at all. Maybe there's hope for you yet."

"You better focus on getting healed up fast. Before I rush over there and kick your ass."

"Promises, promises."

"Exactly."

"Go play nice with Lily." Dillon clicked off.

Cale smiled and shook his head. If he didn't know better, he could place the label of matchmaker on his younger brother.

* * * *

"Is Dillon your only sibling?"

"Yeah. Trust me, he's more than enough."

They'd finished eating at the local cafe and had opted for a walk through the town's sole park as the sunshine and warm fall day called people outside to enjoy the pretty weather before winter arrived soon. He laced his fingers with hers, enjoying the fresh air, her presence by his side, and the lazy Saturday afternoon with only a handful of people milling around—probably owing to the long holiday weekend.

"What was it like growing up? Did you live in the city? Play sports? Make homecoming king in high school?"

Her curiosity seemed endless today. Understandable since they'd crossed the line from guest or friend to lovers in record time. In truth, he never spoke much about himself, cautious by nature and training, more than aware that loose lips sink ships. After years as a SEAL and now as a Wind Warrior, he had quietness and secret holding down to a science.

Yet, he couldn't deny Lily her answers. Most of them. She needed to know more about the man whom she claimed to love.

Love.

She'd tossed the word out before only to be greeted with his muteness on the matter. Stung, she had recovered quickly, promising his lack of confession didn't matter. He didn't buy the forced nonchalance, but he also couldn't open up that much. Not yet. Maybe not ever.

"We grew up on a beef farm. Raised horses, too. Hauled hay in the summer to make money and worked beside our father running the farm. We weren't rich, but worked hard and didn't have a bad life." He recalled those days, working dawn to dusk in the hayfield, the smell of alfalfa almost real as it was way back then. "Dillon and I played football. That's what you did in a small town."

"Homecoming king?"

He grinned and squeezed her hand. "Nope. Not popular enough I suppose."

She smiled up at him. "Your student body was blind."

He shrugged. "Who knows? Not a big deal in the scheme of things. I managed to graduate without regrets."

"And you joined the Navy." She filled in the blank. "Did you always want to be a SEAL?"

"Yeah. Saw a documentary on them as a kid and knew that I wanted to be one of the elite."

"I hear it's beyond tough."

"It has to be. They make sure you're prepared for anything. Your life and the lives of your team members count on it."

Her lips tightened, probably in relation to the inference of death during duty.

"Were you scared?"

They walked a few more steps, then paused to overlook a lake with a small gaggle of geese swimming along on the gentle current. "I'm pretty sure every man had fears at one time or another.

Human nature. You just learn to push past, knowing your team depends upon you."

She craned her head to meet his gaze. "I think you've cornered the market on bravery and courage."

He shook his head. "Not even close." The awe and acceptance in her eyes touched him. He carried scars, physical and psychological, which would never disappear. None of them seemed to matter to Lily. In her eyes, he could be a victorious warrior or a beaten down old soldier and she would still see him in a positive light.

"Ever think what you want to do after you retire from whatever it is you do now?"

He eyed her for a long time, then inclined his head. Yesterday and again this morning, he debated telling her the truth about his occupation. She needed to understand the basics if they were to make their relationship work. Besides, it was only a matter of time before another mission came up. "What I'm going to tell you can get us both killed."

"I'll keep it to myself." Sincerity and promise filled her tones.

"I'm a Wind Warrior now. A team of former special ops men who accept government contracts to go after the nasties hiding out in the US and its neighbors. We're top secret and don't officially exist."

"You take out the bad guys. I already figured out that much."

"Yeah, to put it simply. We stay under radar and have a license to kill. No questions asked."

"So, pretty much like the contracted security teams in foreign countries?" She tilted her head.

"Similar, but on opposite ends of the spectrum. We attack. They defend and protect."

"Just as dangerous if not more so, I imagine," she whispered.

He shrugged.

"What will you do when you retire from the Wind Warriors?"

He blew out a breath. "Haven't thought that far ahead." Glancing down at her, he explained, "You have to understand the mentality of a SEAL or a Wind Warrior. We live in the present because none of us expect much of a future."

She gasped at the statement, spoken so calmly and casually. Her face clouded with worry. "You think you're going to give your life in the line of duty?"

"I used to." He folded her hand tighter in his before lifting hers for a brief kiss. "Now I have something to live for."

"You're good for my ego." Her smile outshone the sun.

"Ditto."

He pivoted and began strolling along the shore once again, automatically raking his gaze over the area, searching for any potential threat, paying attention to even the slightest detail—a habit that saved his ass more times than not.

"Where are your parents now?"

"Still on the farm, last I heard."

"Last you heard? Don't you speak to them?" Lily glanced up at him.

"Not after we nearly came to blows over Rachel. I thought they were unbelievably cruel when they voiced their opinion of her right to her face. Pissed off, I dragged Rachel out of there, vowing to never come back. If I had only listened then."

"Retrospect is always twenty-twenty."

"Yeah."

"So, why haven't you called them up? Obviously, she's out of your life, has been for a while." She stopped and tugged him around to face her.

He didn't care for this particular topic, but Lily proved to be like a dog with a bone. "I've been waiting for them to make the first move."

She snorted. "Let me guess. You're regretful of your actions, but too stubborn to do anything about it."

He cringed at her insightful comment. Somewhat surprised his temper didn't fire, he offered up a vague explanation. "It's more complicated than that."

Lily paused and met his gaze hard. "Let me give you a word of advice from someone who is an orphan. Life is short. Too short. You still have parents who love you, miss you, and grieve because they think their oldest son is lost to them forever all because of an evil witch who's since been crushed by a house." She drew in a breath. "You're the bravest man I've ever known. Suck up your courage, pick up the phone, and throw out an olive branch to your parents."

He heard her words and understood her sentiment, but years of rift between him and his parents stood in the way. "I'll...think about it."

"Good because you don't know what you have until it's gone."

Chapter Twenty

Monday arrived too quickly, forcing Lily back to work. Knowing Cale waited at home for her brightened the whole day and sent her zipping out of the door at the first opportunity. They shared a chuckle when she explained how Carson took one look at her face that morning and slapped a script for birth control pills in her hand. The gesture garnered a blush then just as it had when the incident happened.

"Were the girls good for you today?" Lily asked at dinner.

They both glanced over to the kitty line-up busily eating.

"Yep. They lead a simple life. Eat. Sleep. Play. Repeat."

Lily laughed as she forked another bite of spaghetti that Cale had so thoughtfully prepared while she worked. "It's pretty rough."

Cale's phone rang.

He picked it up, checked the caller ID, and his face turned serious. "Yeah."

Lily tried not to listen in, but she knew who spoke on the other end of the line, based on Cale's hardened expression and the sudden tension in his shoulders. His mouth thinned as he answered in short sentences.

By the time he had finished with the conversation, her appetite had disappeared. Worry replaced happiness as her bubble of perfection burst.

Her gaze lifted to meet his. "Work calls?"

He nodded. "Another mission."

"When do you leave?" She waited with bated breath for his answer.

"Tomorrow at dawn."

Lily's gut clenched. So soon. Too soon. He was leaving and might never return.

"Hey." He reached across the space separating them, using his forefinger to lift her chin. "Do you trust me?"

"Yes." The word came from her very soul.

"Then know I'll come back to you." He kissed her fingertips. "The same way as I trust you'll be waiting for me when I return."

She studied his face. His words sank in. He'd been betrayed before during one of his missions. Add in the fact they'd known one another for a week and she could easily read his meaning and the importance of his belief in her.

"We have to have faith in one another since we're both taking a chance. But understand nothing will keep me away."

A small smile crept on her face. "I'll be waiting for you with open arms."

"How did I get so lucky?" He posed the question while rubbing his hand over her back.

"I'm not sure it's good luck. You've just saddled yourself with a stubborn, set-in-her-ways nurse with a little family of spoiled rotten cats who rule the roost. I live in the middle of nowhere and the nearest civilization boasts two grocery stores, two gas stations, one library, and a post office that doubles as a convenience store."

He chuckled. "Sounds pretty good to me."

As soon as he scooped her up in his arms, he settled his mouth over hers, and proceeded to carry her to the bedroom.

Their time ran short and he knew it.

He made love to her that night with a hint of desperation along with a healthy dose of sensual bonding. She realized this could be their last time together and vowed to make everything extra special—to construct a perfect memory to hold her over for as long as need be. Lily didn't verbalize her concerns. Instead, she poured everything she had into the intimacy with the man she loved, clinging to him even as she cried out his name in a heart-pounding climax.

Chapter Twenty-One

Dawn arrived before she knew it, beautiful and heart-wrenching all the same.

Her ideal life clashed with the real world, leaving her saddened and upset. A week with the man she loved wasn't nearly enough time. Lily's mind told her to be rational. She had always known he had a job that kept him on the move. On the other hand, her heart encouraged her to cling tightly to him, lest he walk out of the door and never return.

"I'll be back. Don't worry."

Lily nodded, tears welling up in her eyes. "I believe you."

He pulled her close, pressing butterfly kisses to her cheeks, soaking up the tears. "Then believe this. I've never had anything as wonderful as you to come home to before. I know you'll be there waiting for me and nothing will keep me from returning to you. Promise."

"I love you, Cale." She hugged him all the tighter.

"I love you, too."

Stunned surprise stilled the hamster wheel inside her mind. The words she longed to hear. She could hardly believe her ears.

Cale grinned down at her, his heart in his eyes. "I mean it. I do love you."

So excited, she nearly bowled Cale over when she threw herself into his arms, squeezing him for all she was worth. "I love you, too. So much."

He chuckled, holding her tight for a moment longer.

She rained kisses over his face, still giddy about his declaration, the moment bittersweet as he finally said the phrase she feared he might never utter to her, then having to immediately ride off into battle once more.

A horn honked behind them.

Coming back to reality, Lily wiped the tears from her eyes, looking up at Cale.

"I'll be back as soon as I can. Take care. You have our numbers in case you need them?"

She nodded. "I'll try not to be a pest." Last night, he had given her a list of important phone numbers but cautioned her that on most jobs they shut down communications for the protection of them and their loved ones. Technology could be easily traced and the men they dealt with had no problem using innocent people for a means to an end. Not only that, but distraction could be deadly. After her experience with Lansing, she understood completely. The thoughts of how close they had all come to a shootout at her house and possible death sent shudders down her spine.

"Never a pest, love." He gave her one final squeeze, a quick kiss, then picked up his gear and strode to the car. Spoon climbed out to open the back. Together they wrangled the large canvas bags into the vehicle, shutting the rear door afterwards.

Cale turned once more, looking at Lily as she stood in the doorway.

She riveted her eyes on him, trying to commit the image to memory.

With a tender smile and wave, he climbed into the car.

Lily watched until she could no longer see the tiny speck of black in the distance. Slowly, she shut the front door and headed for the couch. Tears overflowed once more, her heart aching at the sudden loss. *He'll be back.* That fact gave her a bit of solace, but she couldn't help the onset of loneliness at his departure.

A paw reached up to pat her cheek. Looking over, she saw Hope, sitting beside her with a look of concern in her large expressive eyes. Lily immediately pulled the calico into her lap, taking comfort from Hope's loud purr. The kittens followed suit, Faith and Charity rubbing against her arms, setting their own engines to humming. She soaked in all their affection, happy to have them there. "What would I do without you?"

A few days ago, all she had needed to combat loneliness was her little brood. Now, she needed Cale, too.

A few minutes later, she strode into her bedroom, needing to get ready for work. She paused at the familiar black jacket tossed across the comforter. A bright white paper rested on top. Perplexed, she picked up the note, quietly reading it to herself. *This will keep you warm when I'm not there. Love you and see you soon.*

Lily placed the note back on the bed using both hands to pick up Cale's coat. Pulling it close, she inhaled deeply, easily scenting his woodsy smell imprinted on the fabric. She couldn't help but smile. *I might sniff this thing until the scent wears out.* His consideration and generosity touched her deeply. It was a gift she would wear and treasure, thinking about him each and every time she pulled it on.

* * * *

Promptly at noon, her cell phone rang. Concern immediately flashed through her. Only Carson or Casey ever called and those were fairly few and far between since Casey had delivered Adam and spent all hours of the day and night caring for him. Besides that, she was at work. If Carson needed her, he simply had to walk around the corner to the kitchen where she sat staring at her peanut butter sandwich with little interest.

Dillon's voice carried over the line. "Cale says I'm twitterpated. He said to ask you what it meant."

Lily giggled in relief and in sheer amusement. Leave it to Cale to pester Dillon mercilessly at any given opportunity. "Remember your first crush?"

"Blonde with big boobs in those music videos?"

She snorted. "No, silly Neanderthal. How you felt with your first crush in school." When he remained mute, she continued on with her explanation. "Well, it means you are doting and obsessed or infatuated with someone. You thought of her all the time, planned on when to see her between classes, carried her books, took her to dances, etcetera."

"Oh." Dillon went quiet for a beat. "Maybe I won't kick his butt like I promised after all."

"Uh-huh." She didn't believe that for a minute. "By the way, how's Della?"

"Absolutely wonderful."

She heard the adoration in his tone. No doubt about it, he loved that woman from the top of his head to the bottom of his feet. "Yep, you are definitely twitterpated."

"Hey!"

"I'm just agreeing with Cale." Lily picked at a potato chip. The unexpected call helped ease her loneliness with Cale leaving.

"You miss him." It wasn't a question.

"Yeah. A lot." She sighed into the phone. Worry still ate at her despite her confidence in the team's abilities and Cale's promise to return.

"Don't worry. He's good at what he does."

She nodded then realized he couldn't see it. "I know. It's just hard."

"Yeah. It sucks being on this side." He waited a beat before speaking again. "You love him, huh?"

"More than I ever thought possible." Truth rang with those words.

"Ha! Welcome to the club!"

Lily burst out laughing. She could tell Dillon missed his brother nearly as much as she did. But, together, they would make it through until he returned.

"Lily, really. Call me. Any time you want to talk. I'll be here. Doc won't release me back to work for a few weeks," he offered up, his voice going serious once more.

"I will. Thank you, Dillon. You made me feel better already."

"What are friends for?" With that, he hung up.

Lily clicked her phone off, smiling for the first time since Cale left.

Chapter Twenty-Two

Lily returned to her old routine with work and home chores. The first week proved a challenge, for everywhere she looked a memory of Cale replayed in her head. She missed him more than she could say. But, after some pep talks from Carson, Casey, and Dillon, she slowly accepted his absence as well as any military sweetheart could. Not like there was much choice in the matter. He loved his job and she couldn't insist he find another. No. She loved him for who he was. Taking out the bad guys was simply a part of him.

Sure, she worried that he might never return for one reason or another. Deep down, she knew he would. He meant what he said. She simply needed a bit of faith and trust in order to make it through the days without him.

The no communication rule sucked. She lost count of how many times she wanted to call him up, make sure he was okay, and find out if he would return soon. Dillon coached her through that. More than once he pointed out the reasons not to distract Cale, rational ones she could certainly understand and abide by. It didn't stop her from sending him a quick text now and again, just to let him know she was thinking of him.

"He loves you, Lily. Have no doubt about it," Dillon reassured her one weekend over the phone. "You don't see the changes you made in him. But I do. He'll be back before you know it."

The words gave her strength to carry on for another week, throwing herself into her work. The girls were a huge help, cuddling up on her lap, and sleeping the cold nights lying against her in bed. They might not have been able to speak, but they sure made great listeners.

Lily found another surprise Cale had left for her. About a week after Cale left, Carson handed her a card. "It's from Tiger."

Curious, she quickly opened it, scanning the contents. "A gift card? To the vet?"

Carson smiled down at her. "He wanted to take care of the financial burden of getting the girls spayed and a few other items."

Her eyes began to water. He couldn't have left her a better present. "But it's too much money…"

"No. He said it didn't come close to what he owed you. Besides, he left me something as well." Carson shook his head.

"He did?" Lily couldn't imagine what it could be.

"He knew I wouldn't accept his money, same for you. So, he got crafty. Got you those gift cards. Sent me a complimentary weekend at a bed and breakfast fairly close to Casey's parents."

Lily smiled wide. Leave it to Cale to come up with the perfect thank you for Carson. His in-laws could watch Adam while the doctor and Casey spent some quality alone time together. Something they certainly needed.

"Wait until I see him again." She could think of many ways to show her appreciation. Some of those scenarios quickly turned erotic.

Carson burst out laughing. "Good thing you started taking those birth control pills. I imagine as soon as you see him, you'll drag him to your bedroom, and no one will see either of you for a good week."

Her face heated but she couldn't deny his words.

Chapter Twenty-Three

Two weeks came and went without word from Cale. Lily continued the normal routine of her life, lecturing herself often not to worry. Whispers raced through her mind, flooding her with doubt now and again, before she shoved them away with willpower. It wasn't like his job had set hours and downtime like hers. He said he loved her and would return. Thus, he would.

The girls had been spayed Monday, thanks to Cale's gift. All tolerated the procedure well and had, for the most part, resumed their usual daily activities. Certainly, the surgery hadn't made even a small dent in their appetites. More than once, she considered buying stock in the company that made their cat food. Yet, as much as she commented on the amount and cost of the food, she would do whatever it took to keep providing it for her girls. Never again did she want to see a half-starved cat, desperate to survive. It had broken her heart seeing Hope in that condition and put a smile on her face each time she compared the plump healthy feline to what she had been before. Each homeless animal had such potential if only given the chance. Hope showed her appreciation each and every day, being the most affectionate and loving cat Lily had ever known.

* * * *

Friday evening arrived with a cold snap complete with frigid wind gusts, enough to take her breath away. She hadn't heard the latest weather forecast, but if snow had fallen from the dreary sky, it wouldn't have been a surprise.

A small black SUV sat in her parking place. She didn't recognize the vehicle or the license plate—an out-of-state tag. Unease settled over her as she considered the possibilities and what she should do about each one.

Moments later, fear fled like rain in the desert when she recognized the tall man leaning on the front bumper of the unfamiliar car. Joy and relief engulfed her as Cale glanced up and smiled.

Hastily, she parked the car and jumped out, racing to throw herself into Cale's arms. "I can't believe you're here! I've missed you so much!" She spoke against his ear, holding him tight.

He chuckled, gave her a hard squeeze before pulling back just enough to cover her mouth with his for a quick kiss of greeting. "I missed you, too."

She met his eyes and searched his face. "Are you okay?" Her hand automatically went to his jacket, tunneling under to check for any injuries or wounds.

He shivered as her hands found bare skin on his belly. "Your hands are like icicles."

"I think you told me once that cold hands only made your blood run hotter."

He leaned over enough to rub his nose against hers, tugging her hands from under his shirt. Wrapping his fingers around hers, he tried to warm them. "I said your hands, not cold hands, sugar."

"Oh, was that it?" she teased him, unable to wipe the smile from her face in happiness at seeing him again.

"Uh-huh." He gave her another squeeze and chaste kiss on the mouth. "Let's go inside where it's warm."

Lily grabbed her purse out of the car, along with a small stack of library books, locked it, then returned to Cale.

His gaze settled on the burden in her arms. "Plan on reading a lot this weekend?"

"Well, I did." The heat settled in her cheeks as he pulled the top book off the stack, looking at its cover. For some reason, his knowing that she read juicy romance novels pinged her embarrassment.

He arched an eyebrow after turning over the book to read the back. "Romance, huh?"

She grabbed the book away from him before he could rifle through the pages to the sex scenes. Change of topic was definitely called for. "How long have you been here?"

He shrugged. "A few hours. I already filled the water and checked the fences for you."

"Thanks. I really appreciate that."

"You should." He tugged at her ponytail. "That damn bull didn't cozy up to me nearly like he does you."

She intertwined her fingers with his as they walked the short distance to the back door. "I'm sorry."

"No problem. Stew is ready on the stove. Oh, and I've got a surprise for you." He paused before opening the door, a mischievous grin on his face. Those light blue eyes sparkled.

"A surprise?" Lily couldn't imagine what in the world it could be. He better not have spent more money on her. The vet bill for the girls was more than enough, even if he had a stash of grand wealth at his disposal.

Instead of answering, he opened the back door, ushering her inside.

It took a moment for her eyes to adjust to the brighter light, but as soon as they did, she widened her eyes at the sight.

A large black German shepherd rested on an oversized dog pillow near the couch. Her head came up at their entrance, but she didn't move to greet them.

"Oh, my." Lily walked slowly over, kneeling before the animal. Languidly, she held a hand out to the dog, smiling when a pink tongue flicked out to lick her. Chocolate brown eyes, dull and sad, returned her gaze. Then Lily noticed the shepherd was missing a front leg. Despite that, she appeared in good health with a shiny coat and muscles with a bit of fat covering her bones.

She petted the dog, softly speaking at the same time. "Where did you find her?"

Cale sat down on the floor beside her. "This is Tally."

Charity trotted over to crawl on his lap while Faith took the obstacle course, climbing over the large dog to reach Lily. Tally didn't even blink at the kittens.

"She's a retired Army dog."

"Army dog?" Lily had heard that the military used dogs for tracking and detecting drugs and mines and other things. But she really knew very little about the program.

Cale nodded, picking Charity up to pet her, being extra careful with her shaved tummy. The orange and white spotted kitten purred in delight. "She was trained to sniff out bombs. Spent the last couple of years in Afghanistan."

"Her leg?" Lily stroked between Tally's ears, noting the dog seemed to lean into her hands as if asking for more.

"Roadside bomb. It killed her handler. The shrapnel she took cost her the leg."

"Oh, no." Tears welled up in Lily's eyes at the thought of what the poor animal had been through. "Where did you find her?"

"An old buddy works at the rehab clinic for military dogs in Texas. The Walter Reed for dogs, if you will." He used his free hand to rub along Tally's back. "Anyway, I was close to there and looked him up. He told me about her. How no one would adopt her because she still struggles with post-traumatic stress."

Lily looked away from the dog for the first time, her focus settling on Cale. "Dogs get PTSD?"

"Apparently. It makes sense, if you think about it. Everything that they see and hear during battle." Cale's gaze dropped as he turned his head. Lily reached over to him, patting his thigh. It didn't take a genius to know Cale's mind envisioned something horrific in his past. Wanting to distract him, she inquired more about Tally. "You said she was up for adoption?"

He scratched Charity's ears, then turned to Faith, sharing the attention between the siblings. "The military adopts out the dogs that are no longer able to work. Some go for police dogs, others go to civilians willing to adopt them and care for them."

"You said no one wanted her?" *How could anyone look in those eyes and turn her away?*

"She wasn't a police dog candidate with the missing leg. None of the civilians wanted her either. The hospital did the amputation and gave her extensive rehab, doing everything they could to give her a normal life. But the PTSD seemed to be the issue that turned adopters away. Loud noises send her to hiding, refusing to budge. They say she shakes and is literally terrified. Storms and fireworks are her nightmares."

"Oh. Poor, poor girl." Lily rubbed both hands through the thick fur. "After everything she did there to save lives, now no one will step up and take care of her."

Cale smiled. "Well, someone did."

She pinned him with her gaze. "Who?"

"You."

She blinked. Her mouth opened and shut a couple of times before any words emerged. "Me?"

"Yep." He set the kittens aside, then reached up to cup her cheek. "I couldn't think of anyone better for her. You have a touch, a way with animals."

Lily's mind whirled. "She needs someone with her all the time to build up her confidence and ease her fears. I have to work…"

Cale's finger shushed her. "I've already talked to Mayberry, before the adoption became official. Told them the trainers recommended a quiet home where someone could be with her all the time owing to her fears. He understood. Talked about how many times those dogs saved his life and the lives of those in his unit. He didn't even hesitate, just offered to let her come to work with you each day and hang out in his office. Said it was the least he could do."

Lily nodded, touched once more by the generosity of her boss.

"The cats?"

He gestured at the kittens rubbing all over Tally. "Cat tested and approved."

"Hope?"

"She walked up, smacked Tally on the nose, gave her a royal stare, and then rubbed against her legs. I don't speak feline, but I took that for acceptance after she showed the dog who ruled the house." They both glanced up to find the calico resting on a throw on top of the couch, her front legs tucked under her, in a content and lazy mood.

Lily smiled, picturing Hope doing that very thing. It was no secret the cat ruled her little world. "Okay." She sighed deeply.

For the first time, doubt clouded his expression. "You don't want her?"

She stared down into those big dark eyes, knowing she could never abandon such an animal. "No. It's not that. She just looks so...forlorn. As if she's seen too much, been dealt too many blows in life and has forgotten what happiness and fun are."

Cale shifted closer, wrapping his arm around her shoulder. "That's what drew me to her. That expression. It tore at me. I knew you could bring her back." He pressed a kiss to her temple. "Just like you did with me."

Tears overflowed with his words. Lily turned her head to meet his kiss, breaking apart to wipe at the teardrops. "I love her already. Almost as much as I love you."

His smile lit up the room.

She petted the dog once more, promising she would be well taken care of. "Welcome home, Tally."

Cale stood, pulling Lily up with him. They had to step around the cat toys and a couple of new dog toys before making it to the kitchen. "Let's get you fed."

Using a dipper, he scooped up two big bowls of steamy stew, setting them both on the table. Lily pulled two bottles of water from the fridge and placed them beside the bowls. Both hungrily dug in.

She finished first, raked Cale with her eyes, still shell-shocked and ecstatic that he was there. "Thank you. This is the best gift I could have gotten."

"I can think of a couple of ways to thank me." His voice carried a low husky tone, full of sexual hinting.

"Oh, really?"

"Yeah." He stood, taking her hand in his, kissing the palm before drawing her finger into his mouth, cleaning it with his tongue.

Lily's breath caught at the erotic teasing. Her belly did a slow summersault while parts below clenched in anticipation of what would come next. "You know. It's been a few days. Perhaps I should make sure you still have that belly button, just in case it's disappeared or something."

He laughed before pulling her flush for a deep kiss.

Claws dug into her leg as one of the kittens decided she made a good mountain to climb. At the same time, Tally stuck her cold nose against Cale's groin.

Cale cursed while Lily giggled. "Perhaps privacy is necessary for belly button inspection."

Lily unhooked the troublemaker kitten from her pants, sweetly chastising her while carrying her back to the couch. Cale took charge of Tally, whispering softly to her while digging a chew bone out of a plastic bag sitting on the kitchen counter.

"I think so. Besides, I'm not sure I ever recovered from someone's kitten biting my nipple in search of her breakfast."

"Awwww." She grinned up at him, the memory fresh and funny as ever. "Want me to kiss it again and make it all better?"

"Oh, yeah. Better feed the endless pits before they return for an encore." He rubbed his chest as if the bite still hurt.

With a shake of her head, Lily headed to the kitchen to do just that. Cale moved to fill the dog's food bowl. Feeling his gaze, she turned around, finding his attention locked on her. Quickly, she put the food out, stepped over the cats, and met him in the hall. After taking his hand into hers, she kissed his palm. "I love you, Cale."

"And I love you, too." He tugged her into the bedroom and shut the door firmly behind them.

No sooner had Cale ensured their privacy than Lily began tugging at his shirt, clutching the hem in her fingers and lifting. He took the hint, helping her, before returning the favor. Within a few seconds her clothing lay in a heap on the floor. Cale still wore his jeans even as he stood with a bare chest.

He covered her mouth with his as he used his hands to roam all over her body, leaving sparks in their wake.

Lily kissed him for all she was worth, showing him in the most elemental way possible how much she missed him and welcomed him back. She reached out, unbuttoning his jeans, slipping her hand in to find the object of her search. His erection jumped with the slightest brush of her fingers. Unable to help herself, she shimmied the jeans down his hips, letting them fall to his feet. Following them down, she knelt before him, grasping his cock in hand. She looked up at his face for an instant then reached out with her tongue, licking over the tip in a sultry kiss.

He groaned deep, but his gaze never wavered.

With more confidence, she focused on her task at hand, slipping her mouth over him, licking and suckling, moving as deep as she dared before reversing her maneuvers, elating with each jerk and moan from Cale, signaling that her limited skills met his approval.

He reached down to cup her cheek, gently pushing her away. "I can't take any more."

Lily looked longingly at the arousal jutting in front of her and wet her lips, not ready to give up her succulent prize. Just as she leaned forward to take him inside her mouth, he scooped her up and carried her to the bed.

"You can do that later, sugar. Right now, I want to be inside you." Cale's low tones and words sent her belly on another deliciously slow summersault.

Upon laying her down in the center of the large bed, he followed her down, raining kisses over her body, before focusing his attentions on her breasts, while he spread her legs and sought her innermost femininity. She welcomed his invasion, writhing in a desperate need for more. She explored his chest and back with enthusiasm and eagerness then, reaching down to grasp his blatant arousal, ran her fingers back and forth over his sensitive flesh.

Cale groaned then pulled back, nibbling her inner thighs while staring at her juicy center.

Lily tensed. She recalled the last time he had showered such attentions on her, sending her into paradise in short order. But she had worked all day long, hadn't showered since early morning, hadn't changed her underwear.

As if understanding her uncertainty, Cale soothed her. "Shhh." Leaning in, he licked across her outer folds. "Mmmmm. Such sweet nectar. Share with me, love." He urged her thighs farther apart, used his fingers to open her for his tasting.

Lily gasped at the delightful sensations centered on Cale's administrations with his talented tongue. She dug into the cushiony surface, needing something stable to cling to in light of the near violent rapture beginning to fire inside her, even as she widened her legs, needing him closer and deeper.

Two fingers slipped inside while he licked around, then over her highly sensitive clit. A whimper escaped her lips. "Please." Her body demanded more than his teasing.

Cale lifted, once again hovering over her. Upon wrapping her in his arms, he quickly rolled them both over, switching their positions. He reclined on his back with Lily perched on top.

She looked down at him and smiled in remembrance. While different from sitting on his lap, the theory remained the same. She called the shots. The thought sent a shiver down her spine as well as a twinge of uncertainty. He'd helped her before. This time she would be on her own.

As if sensing her hesitation, Cale reached out to cup a breast, tenderly squeezing and molding, brushing his thumb over the nipple. "Ride me, love. Just like before."

The words and his half-mast bedroom eyes forged her confidence. Adjusting her position, she scooted to align their hips. He assisted by bracketing her hips with his hands, encouraging her to move astride. Once she found the angle, he released one hand to grasp his cock, guiding it to her center.

Lily watched his face, then slowly settled over him, taking him deep inside her body. Her core welcomed him back with abundant dampness, ensuring ease of entry.

He clenched her hips, but otherwise, he remained still, allowing her to set the pace. After a pause to catch her breath, she began experimental movements up and down as well as a gentle rolling motion, learning the location of hotspots for both of them.

Cale roamed her body, always returning to her modest breasts, before venturing out once more. More than once, he dipped between their bodies, his fingers glistening from the procured moisture.

She continued this slow and easy rhythm until Cale took control once more. He pulled her down hard to meet his counterpoint thrusts, increasing their speed, and intensity. Lily threw her head back, allowing him to direct her motions, needing more, deeper, and harder. She braced her hands against his chest, giving her purchase for his pounding movements.

"Come for me, Lily." He removed one hand from her hip, slid over to where their bodies met. He found her clit with his deft fingers and plucked.

The growing tension escalated immediately. One more rub of the sensitive area sent her over the edge with a quiet cry. Contractions locked Cale deep within her body as wave after wave of ecstasy shot through her. Her body massaged and milked him as she pressed firmly to him, soaking up every nuance of sexual excitement.

Cale pounded against her for another few strokes, bucking his hips frantically, before clamping her tightly against his groin, ensuring his erection remained buried deep throughout his climax. Deep moans and a few shudders racked his body before he relaxed once more.

Lily wilted, draping over his chest, valiantly trying to catch her breath, still feeling the minor spasms deep inside where Cale joined with her. He lightly rubbed her back before wrapping his arms around her, holding her close.

She nuzzled his pecs before nipping him lightly with her teeth, smiling to herself when his cock jerked inside her. Focusing, she tightened her vaginal muscles while licking across his nipple. Despite the recent exertion, she felt energized, revved up, eager for the next bout of lovemaking.

"Damn, vixen," Cale muttered against her shoulder.

Lily sat up enough to look into his face. She grinned wickedly as she performed another hip roll.

Cale tensed under her, his large hands easily holding her locked in place. "You can kill a man like that."

"Good thing tigers have nine lives."

He chuckled warmly, smiling up at her.

"Welcome home, Cale." Lily leaned down to kiss him lightly on the lips, snuggling into his large, warm body.

"This is home. Because of you, love."

Epilogue

They pulled into the long gravel driveway, heading toward the single story brick house surrounded on all sides by pastures and hayfields. Memories assailed him even though it had been years since he had visited his parents or their home. Familiar fields where he and Dillon had played baseball and chase. Where livestock had grazed for as long as he could remember. Mom would place a pitcher of sun tea out on the porch early so it would be ready for lunch. They hauled hay in the summer, helped feed that same hay to the livestock in winter when over a foot of snow closed roads and school for the day.

This was home.

Dillon had called them earlier in the week, serving as a go-between once more. His parents wanted a small family get-together with their sons. Not since before the divorce had that happened. The time had come to lay the past behind them and step ahead into the future, which included reuniting with his parents, or at least trying to. Dillon was right in that regard, although he didn't dare tell his younger brother that. His head was big enough already.

Unfortunately, Dillon had also told Lily. She'd lectured him more than once on the importance of parents in his life, even as an adult, making him feel guilty when she mentioned how much she wished her mother was still alive, so he could meet her. She didn't nag. It wasn't her style. Besides, those stories of love and missing her departed mother had proved much more effective in relaying her message. They'd cut through his defenses as nothing else could.

He'd tried to ignore her, but she had placed Operation Parent Reunion at the top of her to do list. She'd cajoled, lectured, sweet-talked, and had finally swayed him with all her prodding. He couldn't deny her anything she wanted. That fact would terrify him with anyone else. Lily possessed an innate honesty and compassion that earned and kept his trust while her unquestioned love made him strive to keep her happy. She did so much for him, gave him so much. He sought ways to repay her for all those little moments of joy only she could provide.

Cale had sucked it up and phoned his parents a few days before. They had only spoken for a few minutes, but his mother had sounded hopeful and excited to hear from him. His father had concurred, in his gruffer manner. Since his father had spent his early medical career as an Army physician before leaving to pursue private practice, gruffness and orders were simply a part of the man. It had been that way as long as he could remember.

When his mother had invited him out the following weekend, he'd immediately agreed, promising to bring Lily along. As if he could leave her at home. Lily would've moped even as she understood his reasons.

However, his mother had refused to be denied the opportunity to meet Lily after Dillon had sung her praises to them. His father, short on words, would expect an introduction, wanting to assess Lily for himself.

It was a start and he really hoped a springboard for the future. He had missed his family, more so as he realized the important things in life were more than a paycheck and a sniper rifle. Dillon had filled in the gaps over the past few years, but now he wanted more.

Carson had offered to look after the girls while they were gone for an extended weekend. Lily had fretted about leaving them alone—after all, none of them had ever spent a night without her. But Casey had reassured her that between her and Carson, the cats would be well cared for and wouldn't miss a single meal.

Of course, Tally came along for the trip. The German shepherd had made great progress in her shyness and fears, blossoming under Lily's patient touch. She now ran and played, chasing a ball until whose arm grew tired. Though still frightened of loud noises, a spark had returned to her eyes, replacing the dull, hopeless expression of before. Cale placed the credit squarely on Lily. With love, she showed the dog that happiness and fun still existed, she only needed a bit of trust and belief.

Lily refused to leave her alone, even with Carson looking in on them. One thunderstorm without someone there could send Tally backwards, she'd argued, losing all the hard-won progress. Lily made it a requirement, even if they needed to stay at a local hotel. Luckily, his parents understood and extended the offer to Tally, as well. They'd always had dogs growing up, so it wasn't a big inconvenience to them. Animals were the center of his parents' life on the ranch. One well-behaved dog following alongside could easily be accepted, even happily welcomed.

Nearing the house, Lily discovered a small group of horses standing near the east fence, close to the driveway. "Oh, my. Look! Aren't they gorgeous?"

No sooner had Cale cut the engine on the SUV, than Lily threw the passenger door open. She dashed over to the fence, already talking to the small herd that quickly gathered around her, curious and probably looking for treats. A bold colored stallion nudged to the front, stretching his head over the fence. His white hide with brown spots sparkled in the morning sun. As he watched, Lily reached out, scratching the horse's forehead as he leaned in for more, ears and body relaxed, a look of equine contentment if he'd ever seen one.

Cale could only shake his head—whether bulls or stallions, Lily turned them all into big babies.

The squeak of a screen door drew his attention. His parents walked toward him, both wearing jeans and sweatshirts.

"Cale! I'm so happy to see you!" His mother hugged him tightly before stepping back, beaming at him with a wide smile. Her dark hair bore more silver steaks than the last time he had seen her, but she remained as always, beautiful and dignified.

His father offered his hand, grinning when Cale shook it without hesitation. "Good to see you, son."

"You, too, Dad." Cale noticed his father's hair held more gray and his jeans had probably increased a belt notch, but otherwise, he had changed as little as his mother.

He searched his father's eyes, trying to locate the harbored resentment and anger. If there was any, he couldn't detect it.

"Is that Lily?" His father gestured toward the pasture where she stood petting horses with Tally sitting dutifully beside her. The dog had bolted out of the car right behind Lily, never wanting Lily out of her sight. A stuffed turtle dog toy hung from either side of her mouth. Tally had latched onto the thing as soon as Lily had brought it home a couple of weeks before. Since then, she'd carried it everywhere she went and slept with it every night. Her version of a security blanket, they'd decided.

His father's question didn't really surprise him. Although he had spoken to his parents a couple of times recently, Dillon remained the major source of information between the two parties. Obviously, his little brother had filled them in about Lily and their relationship. Knowing Dillon's penchant for yapping, Cale would expect his parents to know pretty much everything about Lily and how he felt about her.

"Yeah, that's her. The one enamored with your herd stallion."

"She's got a good eye for studs." His father answered shrewdly. A low snort followed.

"Hal!" His mother lightly smacked her husband in the arm. "Good grief."

Cale chuckled, noting his father did as well. He relaxed his shoulders, feeling for the first time that things just might work out between them. It was a good start, at least. Much better than he'd feared.

"I've got to get the boxes out of the car."

"Boxes?" His mother shot him a look of bewilderment. "I told Dillon we didn't need anything. Just to bring yourselves."

"Lily wanted to cook something and bring it with us, insisting we couldn't just show up without a contribution to the dinner table. She decided she could bake better than cook and spent hours figuring out what to prepare. We brought homemade bread, cinnamon rolls, and a couple of pies."

"Oh, my. That's enough to fatten everyone up for winter." She brought a hand up to rest on her chest.

Cale grinned. "Yeah, she kept hoping that Dad wouldn't turn up diabetic before we arrived, just in case."

His father rolled his eyes at that, while he continued to watch Lily pamper the stallion.

As if feeling eyes on her, Lily turned to them. Blushing prettily, she slowly walked in their direction, chewing on her bottom lip the whole way.

"Seems a bit nervous," his father pointed out.

Cale followed his father's gaze. "She's a bit like the shepherd. Brave, dedicated, loyal, and would lay down her life for someone she loves. For all that, she's a little uncertain of new people and their acceptance of her." His words trailed off as she stepped up.

After confiding to Lily about his past, Cale had understood her hesitancy in meeting his parents. She was so afraid they wouldn't like her. She'd told him more than once that she didn't want to ruin his second chance, but insisted he go visit, mend the old hurts, and regain parental support. He'd reassured her over and over again that they would simply adore her, just like everyone else. Everyone knew that to be true but Lily. Hopefully, today would prove all her fears unfounded.

He wrapped an arm around her waist. "Mom. Dad. This is Lily. Lily, these are my parents, Hal and Linda."

"We're so happy to finally meet you," Linda gushed as Lily shook hands with both of his parents.

"Me, too."

Cale pulled her against his side. "Maybe we should get those baked goods?"

Lily grinned widely. "Oh, good idea." She stepped after him, then paused to look back at his parents. "I hope you find something you like. I wasn't sure what to bring, so I just brought a little of everything."

Cale pulled the biggest cardboard box from the back of the SUV after handing Lily the smaller one.

Linda peeked inside Lily's box. "Oh, my. It looks like you prepared to feed an army."

"Well, Cale did say Dillon was coming," Lily tossed out tartly, following his mother toward the house.

Chuckles filled the air. It was no secret Dillon ate like the world would soon run out of food and he intended to stock up before that happened. Only his high metabolism and constant exercise prevented him from carrying an extra hundred pounds in body weight.

Linda led Lily to the side door, holding it open for the younger woman. Tally hopped along on her three legs with ease of practice, keeping pace with her mistress. She, too, snuck through the open door with her ever-present green toy, wagging her tail at his mother in thanks.

Cale started after them only to be stopped by his father's voice.

"Son." One hand combed through his dark hair while he sucked in a breath. "Look, I know we've had our issues in the past."

Cale nodded, his gut clenching with anticipation of what would come next. He really wanted this to work. His father was his mentor, his hero when he was younger. The black hole caused by his ex-wife had torn a wound inside that begged for repair.

"I like that girl. Anyone that can take on an ornery, old cuss and make him happy as a dog with a big bone is all right in my book." He slapped Cale on the back. His smile extended into his eyes, making the blue irises, so like his own, glimmer.

Leave it to his father to be most impressed with Lily's ability to soothe the nastiest-tempered beast. He assumed his father spoke of the Appaloosa stud in the pasture. But, the twinkle in his father's eye made him realize that his father could easily have meant him, too.

He shook his head at the backhanded compliment, returning his father's amused grin. *You have to read between the lines with him.* Relief flowed over him at the warm reception. He never knew how much his father's acceptance meant to him until he lost it. Now, thanks to Lily, he had it back. It couldn't have been better in his opinion. Old hurts still remained, but he pushed past them, just thankful that his father had the gumption to forgive him.

"Take my advice and marry that one."

Cale blew out a breath. "I'm thinking about it, Dad. Really thinking about it."

"Good to know. I always knew you were smart." With a light smack on the back, his father guided him toward the house.

Perhaps his father was right after all. She had wormed her way under his skin, into his heart, and each day made him smile and crave those sweet hands on his body.

Cale had been a true beast of a man before Lily had tamed him with sheer kindness, compassion, and something more. So much more.

He'd gleefully spend the rest of his life in the glow of their love. For dreams occasionally do come true.

About the Author

Growing up in the Midwest, I began reading romance novels in high school, immediately falling in love with the genre, to the point where I decided to write professionally for a career. However, that dream splattered against a brick wall, resulting in a quick death in my first writing class in college when my professor told me bluntly that I wasn't any good at it. I shifted gears quickly, and left my writing dreams behind, eventually settling on becoming a nurse.

A few years back, I stumbled across a fan-fiction writing site on a favorite author's webpage. I began to read stories others wrote, not only making some wonderful close friends from the experience, but also, really learning to write for the very first time. Here I was able to share short stories, practice my writing skills, and truly develop into a writer. More than that, the experience allowed me to revitalize my dream, as I rediscovered joy in writing. Now, I spend my days off with my alpha male characters, quick witted heroines, and see how much trouble everyone can get into.

When I'm not working or writing, I enjoy working in the garden, canning, and seeing my backyard as a living canvas for my whimsical landscaping, and, of course, reading romance novels.

Cheyenne Meadows loves to hear from readers. You can find her contact information, website details and author profile page at http://www.totallybound.com.

Totally Bound Publishing

www.ingramcontent.com/pod-product-compliance
Lightning Source LLC
Chambersburg PA
CBHW020422180626
46812CB00003B/1101